Heritage Series – Volume II

Susan Diane Black Blackmon

This is a work of fiction. All of the characters,
organizations, and events portrayed in this novel are
either products of the author's imagination or are used
fictitiously.

Library of Congress Control Number: 2022923611

Celey – Heritage Series – Volume II
by Susan Diane Black Blackmon.

Hardbound ISBN: 978-1-959980-01-8
Paperback ISBN: 978-1-959980-00-1

Independently published by
Susan Diane Black Blackmon UNITED STATES
Graham, Texas, USA, 76450
www.whispersfromthepast.net

Background cover photo courtesy of:
David Eick and Dawn Jones
Descendants of Worth Cyrus Neff 1850-1933

I dedicate this story to my sister, Linda. Thank you for always being my cheerleader.

About the Author

In 1976, I fell in love with genealogy. I have my eighth-grade History teacher to thank for that. She assigned an autobiographical project requiring us to complete a pedigree chart. "The Tale of the Beautiful Princess - Or Everything You Always Wanted to Know About Me, But Were Afraid to Ask" resulted in two A+ grades.

Over the next forty-six years, I amassed a collection of thousands of photographs and documents related to my family heritage. Most importantly, I spent countless hours listening to my

MamMaw (grandmother) and my great-aunt tell stories about my ancestors.

During that time, I compiled several books on genealogy and "published" them at the local print shop. In 2015 I published my first set of books through Amazon, and the second set in 2017.

In September of 2022, I completed a project that had been the dream of a cousin. He had always wanted to write a book based on Civil War letters he inherited from his great-grandmother by way of an aunt. The letters and other memorabilia "lived" in a pillow case inside a chair cushion for many years. My cousin passed away before he could realize his dream, and I had the honor of presenting these 158-year-old treasures in a format allowing the entire family to enjoy them. Hot on the heels of publishing this work came my sixtieth birthday.

Turning sixty may have been the reason I allowed my older sister to shove me out of my wheelhouse of genealogy and into writing the book *Emma*. Older sisters can be pretty bossy, and this one has a sharp stick that she likes to poke me with, metaphorically.

She kept encouraging me to try my hand at writing a book. I intended to write a short story based on our great-grandmother and a few events in her life. I had planned on a handful of pages, and it would be back to my next genealogy project. Two weeks later, I presented her with a 264-page rough draft of *Emma*. She read it, insisted I let other family members and friends read it, and the next thing you know, here we are.

Table of Contents

Prologue

Arkansas 1851 –

A slow rain fell as Celey walked from the graveyard, her tears mingling with the tears of God.

In the distance, she saw Tom Anderson. Her heart raced, and her anger flared. *How dare that rotten scoundrel show his face here!*

Chapter 1

Harrison and his twin brother, Ezekiel, were born in Ohio in 1797. About 1810, their father, Captain Jacob Dobbs, had moved his large family down the Ohio River to Illinois and the Old Northwest Territory, settling near William's Ferry.

The following year they moved out onto the prairie near the northern limits of White County, and for a time, they lived in peace with the Indians.

In 1813, Harrison's oldest brother, Amos, had herded their hogs and those of nearby families to an area where they could feed on the mast and fatten up for butchering. Amos had built a small camp near the creek, and he and his dog, Old Beve, settled in.

When Amos didn't return home as expected, their father searched for him and found the Indians had killed him. They had mounted his severed head on a stake and burned his mutilated body. The stock, his pony, and Old Beve were gone. His father had buried Amos where he found him; after that, the place had been called Dobbs' Prairie.

Fearing the Indians were on the warpath, Jacob moved his family to Captain McHenry's blockhouse. Time passed, and no further word came of trouble with the Natives, so the family moved back to their little settlement.

While hunting one day, Jacob and a group of men from his old command had come across a small band of Indians near the Little Wabash River. The men recognized Amos' horse and saw Old Beve lying nearby, so they quickly surrounded the group. Jacob could speak their language and questioned the leader about the pony. The Indian told him the horse was his, having won it in battle, and mimicked the terrified boy's pleas for his life. He told Cap't. Dobbs, they were at peace now. Jacob, being a man of few words, said, "<u>You</u> may be at peace, but I am not!"

He quickly killed two Indians, and his men killed the others. As one tried to escape, Jacob 'hissed' Old Beve, who leaped on the Indian in the river, drowning him. The men returned to the settlement, leading Amos' pony with Old Beve, trotting alongside.

Not long afterward, they had moved closer to the village of Carmi, Jacob's wife fearing retribution from the Indians. It was in Carmi that Harrison met Clarissa Davis.

Clarissa was a petite young woman with sparkling eyes and a quick wit. Harrison was smitten the moment he met her. Following a brief courtship, they were married in December of 1817.

After losing their first two children in childbirth, Harrison and Clarissa moved to the Shawneetown Riverport. There was a doctor there for Clarissa and plenty of work for Harrison. Celey was born in April of 1827 on a beautiful Spring night. As a little girl, her mother had told her that her name meant 'heavenly light.'

Harrison and his brother Ezekiel loaded their families into wagons in the mid-eighteen-thirties and made their way into Western Arkansas. Ezekiel settled in the Southern tip of Crawford County and Harrison near the Poteau River at Waldron in Scott County.

Arkansas was a new state, and the pioneers who settled there were isolated from civilization, but Harrison and Ezekiel thought it was worth the hardship. Never had they seen such abundance. Wild fruits, muscadine grapes, blackberry, and huckleberry, lined the river banks, and the forest teemed with deer, turkey, and all manner of game. Immense herds of buffalo roamed the prairie.

For all the wonders and bounty it possessed, Scott County was a wild region. There were no churches, and the circuit preacher only made it to their town every few months. The settlers would meet in their homes and read the Good Book, but there was a significant disregard for the Sabbath.

Harrison and Clarissa's family had grown to include two sons, Levi and Jackson, and a second daughter, Amanda.

Chapter 2

Scott County, Arkansas – circa 1843

Celey Dobbs and her younger sister, Amanda, made their way down the main street of Waldron. The town was growing, but Celey was still determining if that was good. Instead of becoming more civilized, it had become wilder and more dangerous. The girls rarely came to town without Father. Mother worried that it wasn't safe for young ladies. Today she had reluctantly allowed them to go, giving them a firm talking to and making them promise they would stay together and not speak to anyone except Mrs. Chambers, the storekeeper's wife.

Mother would never have let them come to town alone if she hadn't needed a tin of Black Draught salve.

Their brother, Jackson, had a Bitter Orange thorn in his hand, and the wound had festered. Mother had tried to dig it out with her needle, but it was too deep. She'd wipe some Black Draught on it and cover it with a clean rag, and the thorn would pop right out in a few days.

Celey gripped Amanda's hand tightly as they walked into the store. Leaning against the counter, smoking his pipe, was Tom Anderson. He had a reputation, and it wasn't good. Father refused to do business with him, saying, "He was in league with the Devil." Celey wished Father was with them now.

Amanda was fascinated by all the merchandise. Everywhere she looked, something new caught her eye. Celey tried her best to get what they needed and get out before Anderson noticed them, but Amanda would not hurry.

Celey had paid for their purchase, and they were just about to step outside when Tom Anderson blocked their way and said, *You're the Dobbs girls.* Celey kept her eyes down and said softly *Yes, sir. Please, excuse us, sir.* Mother had taught her to be polite, no matter who it was. As she tried to step past him, he spoke again in a menacing voice; *You better tell your papa that he's gonna be right sorry if he don't sell me that land.*

Celey's dark brown eyes grew wide, and her heart sped up. The man scared her. She tried again to step past him, but he blocked her way. She glanced around, looking for an escape, but could find none. Not knowing what else to do, she turned to retreat into the store and ran into someone standing directly behind her. Her panic grew, thinking it must be one of Anderson's cronies. She started to call out to Mr. Chambers, then she heard a deep voice say, *Anderson, move along; you're blocking these ladies' way.* She raised her eyes and saw two young men standing, shoulder to shoulder, eyes stern, as they waited for the man to move.

Tom stood for a moment more, muttered a curse, and stalked away. Celey breathed a quick *Thank you,* then hurried through the door, anxious to reach their wagon. One of the men laid his hand on her arm, and she thought maybe they'd stepped from the frying pan into the fire.

Miss Dobbs. My name's Daniel Tilman, and this is my brother, Henry. Ladies, I'd be obliged if you let us see you home. Celey wondered what they had gotten into now. *See, Miss, Tom Anderson's a scoundrel, and I would rest easier knowin' you ladies were safe to home.* Amanda was shocked when Celey agreed and allowed him to help her into their wagon and drive them home.

Celey knew Mother and Father would not be happy about her allowing a stranger to drive them, but honestly, she thought they were more like guardian angels. The encounter with Mr. Anderson had shaken her.

Mother was hanging her laundry outside when the wagon pulled into the yard. She was shocked to see her daughters in the wagon with a strange man -  another man was riding a horse and leading one. Before Mother could say a word, Celey had scrambled down over the wheel and was at her side, explaining what had happened and assuring her Mother that the men had rescued them from Mr. Anderson. Clarissa was sorry that she'd let the girls go into town but was certainly grateful to the men for watching out for them.

Later, when Father and the boys came in from the field, Mother told them about what had happened. Levi wanted to give 'ole Anderson' what for, but Father told him to hush and get washed for supper.

Clarissa asked what Harrison thought he should do; he shook his head. Harrison hated violence, but that reprobate had to be dealt with before his boy did something they would all regret later. He couldn't stand by and let Anderson harass his daughters.

Chapter 3

Jefferson Tilman had brought his family to Scott County from Missouri in 1836. When they arrived, Arkansas was a newly annexed state, just months old. He and his wife, Alsey, had two boys, Daniel and Henry, and a daughter, Alice. He had always had a bit of wanderlust, and when he heard what a good land this was, he had to see it for himself. Little did he know, it would one day be his biggest regret.

The Tilmans had a farm a few miles east of Waldron. The little town was still wild, and there was a great deal of wickedness. There was no school, so the mothers taught their children their letters and sums around the kitchen table.

Jefferson and his boys had worked hard to build a sturdy log cabin for the family before the first winter set in. The boys cut timber from the forest on their land and cleared the homeplace while Jefferson hewed the logs and notched them. Working together, they soon enjoyed the cozy cabin's warmth while the winter winds howled outside.

In the evenings, the family would sit near the fireplace, and Jefferson would tell them stories of fighting with the Indians against the British and the trip from Kentucky to Ohio and Missouri. When the stories ran dry, the boys would sit around the table and discuss having farms of their own. Alice would help their ma with mending and whisper to her about the boys in town. Each night before they went to bed, Jefferson would take down his Bible and read a passage, then the family would pray together.

Most of their neighbors were hardworkin', God-fearin' folks, happy to lend a hand when need be. But every place on earth had a few bad seeds, and Waldron was no exception.

Daniel and Henry came in from town, and as they were unloading the wagon, they told their pa about Tom Anderson harassing the Dobbs girls. Having had run-ins with the man, Jefferson knew Tom tried his best to bully anyone he could. Anderson had a nasty streak in him. Most folks were content with what the good Lord had given them. Tom wanted his portion and then some. Lately, he had been trying to strong-arm the farmers in their neighborhood into selling their land to him. Jefferson knew that Harrison Dobbs had turned him down cold, as had most of the others. He had heard that 'Old Man' Crenshaw finally gave in after his barn mysteriously burned down. Crenshaw took his money and moved his family up to Fort Smith.

Jefferson had no intention of selling. He and his family were happy on their patch of land, and he intended on being there for a spell. He warned Alsey and Alice not to go into town without one of the men folk. Anderson and his bunch had not done anything but bully folks so far, but it was best not to take chances.

After supper, Henry and Daniel went out to check the livestock. The night was so mild that they stopped to lean on the fence rail and stare up at the stars. The sky was a deep blue, and the tiny lights twinkled brightly. After a few moments, Henry said, *That Dobbs girl sure has pretty eyes, twinkly like them stars.* Daniel laughed; *You sweet on that girl, little brother?* Henry gave him a cuff on the shoulder, and the brothers headed into the barn.

Later, as Daniel lay in his bed, the confrontation with Anderson replayed in his mind. He didn't understand how the man could be so mean. He knew that some men were just bullies; from his experience, they were usually cowards.

His pa had told him that Anderson had been pressuring him to sell the farm. Tom had done the same with other neighbors. The man had more land than anyone else in the county; why did he want more? Daniel thought about the Dobbs girls and how frightened they had looked when Anderson had blocked their way. He had noticed the man bothering them and saw him whisper something to the older girl. He wished he knew what it was.

Daniel thought she looked just like an animal caught in a snare when she ran into him. Her eyes had been wild with fear. He knew that he would not feel easy until those girls were safely home. They should have been there with their father; Waldron was a rough town.

As sleep claimed him, Daniel envisioned the darkest pair of brown eyes he recollected.

Chapter 4

Tom Anderson was the largest landowner in Scott County. The way he looked at things, the man with the most land could control the county, and that's just what he meant to do. Anderson had come down from Missouri in 1834 and staked his claim. He'd been here longer than most, and he'd run off those he didn't like. No one challenged him much, and he wasn't above helpin' folks disappear that crossed him.

He'd done a little of everything, not all of it legal. He had well-placed friends where he needed them. If things got sticky, Anderson could count on them to smooth it over. He handled the dirty work, and Laben Fondren and Gus Yates provided him with an alibi. Tom always knew some scallywag he could blame if their actions required something not entirely lawful. This arrangement worked well for everyone *except* their victims.

The truth was, Tom had liked it better before all the do-gooders had started showin' up. It seemed like every time he turned around, some long-nosed bitty was squawkin' about sin and him burnin' in hell.

Anderson owned a livery stable and freight company and had his hand in the till of most of the businesses in town. Having control of what supplies came into the county and went out, he could force the prices up or down as suited him.

Most folks didn't realize that Tom and Asa Chambers at the mercantile worked together. Between them, they had managed to put away a tidy sum of money. Anderson would buy a load of stolen goods from a cohort in Ozark, then sell low to Chambers. The storekeeper would then mark up the prices and complain about the high freight cost making everything more expensive. The unsuspecting town folk had nowhere else to purchase the goods they needed, so they paid the prices. The two men split a hefty profit with this arrangement. Several times, folks had declared they couldn't afford the high cost of dry goods any longer and had sold their land at pennies on the dollar to move somewhere else. Interestingly enough, Anderson was always there, ready to 'help them out in their time of need' by buying their property for much less than it was worth. He'd acquired several hundred acres of the best farm and timberland in the county; still, he wanted more and was hell-bent on getting it.

A bunch of high-and-mighty farmers east of Waldron was in the way of what he was after next. He hadn't figured out exactly how to get them to sell, but he was willing to have his accomplices do whatever it took. Crenshaw had gone easy enough when his barn caught fire –Anderson thought <u>maybe</u> he needed to turn up the heat.

There was a creek running through the west side of Tom's land, but the east side didn't have a water source that belonged to him. Jefferson Tilman had a natural spring on his place that fed a creek. That creek ran across Harrison Dobbs' farm and onto Tom's land. Most folks would have been satisfied to have that, but Anderson wasn't most.

How Tom saw it, if he didn't own the water, Tilman or Dobbs could stop him from using it. He would have done that, and he judged everyone by his actions. Besides, he had big plans for that spring water, and he didn't want them nosing around.

Anderson had figured getting rid of Harrison Dobbs wouldn't be hard. Tom considered Dobbs yellow and thought that if he badgered him and his family enough, Dobbs would gladly sell – so far, nothing had worked. Anderson thought about the Dobbs girls; they weren't hard to look at, even if they were prissy things. That dark-eyed one was pert-near-growed; he might steal a kiss before he finished with her old man.

And as for Daniel Tilman, Tom owed <u>that</u> interfering cuss a good thrasin'. Tilman and his brother had stuck their noses in Tom's business too many times, and he was itchin' to make them pay. Getting them and their pa off their farm would be more complicated than Dobbs. Jefferson Tilman wasn't as peaceful; he was holier-than-thou, but Tillman raced headlong at conflict where Dobbs tried to avoid it. The key to everything was Tilman; if he and his sons were out of the way, it would be easy for Tom to get rid of Dobbs.

Chapter 5

Daniel Tilman was twenty-three years old. He and his younger brother, Henry, had a dream. He and Henry had been doing odd jobs any chance they got and had just about saved enough to buy eighty acres from their pa. They would get a crop in, and once they got their harvest to market, they'd build a cabin and barn. The brothers would 'batch' for a couple of years until they made enough money to build a second cabin and barn. Neither of them had a special girl, and they weren't in a hurry to settle down. There was plenty of time for that after they had everything in order. Pa had told them they could pay him over time, but they agreed that the land wouldn't be theirs until they paid for it in full. Besides, there were too many unexpected expenses when you were a farmer.

They could continue living with Pa and Ma until they built a cabin. Daniel figured that by the time he was twenty-eight, they'd have things pretty well in order, and he'd start thinking about a wife and family. He told himself he didn't have time for that right now. What with working with Pa and their odd jobs and pretty soon their farm, there wasn't time for courtin'. In a few years, he would be ready to support a family, and then he could look around and see who interested him.

When he was hitching up the team to head into town, his sister, Alice, had asked if she could tag along; she needed some thread from the mercantile. Daniel enjoyed Alice's company; she wasn't flighty and silly like most girls her age.

When Alice turned sixteen, the family had given her a Hope Chest  that he, Pa, and Henry had built from cedar out of their forest. Ma had embroidered tea towels as her gift. Alice was finishing a quilt that would go into the chest along with the towels and other items she either made or Ma had passed down. When she was old enough to marry, in a few years, she would have a start on setting up her household. Daniel had often thought that men should have a chest as well. They could put tools and seeds and such in it.

On the ride to town, Alice and Daniel chatted about the farm he and Henry were close to buying, and they each shared their dreams for their future. While Daniel's were of seeds and stock, Alice's were about a young man living on the outskirts of Waldron, Caleb Reed.

Alice had met Caleb at one of the open-air camp meetings a circuit-riding preacher had held last Spring. On the last day of the week-long meeting, the ladies had dinner on the ground, and most of the local folks had a day of good food and a rare chance to visit with neighbors.

Daniel had known his sister was sweet on Caleb and suspected her desire to go to town had more to do with the possibility of running into <u>him</u> than needing thread for her quilt. Whatever her motive, Daniel was enjoying her company.

As they drew close to the Dobbs farm, they noticed the women working in the garden, and Alice waved and called out to them. Daniel realized that his little sister craved the company of others, something she didn't often have with no formal church or school. He pulled up on the reins, stopping the wagon in the yard to allow Alice a short visit.

Daniel wasn't paying close attention to their conversation; he was going over the list of items he needed from the mercantile in his mind. His head snapped up when he heard Alice say, *Oh, Daniel won't mind a bit if Celey rides along with us.*

While Celey dashed inside to get her bonnet and her mother's list, Mrs. Dobbs thanked Daniel. *It's just such a blessing that you are taking her into town. Harrison has forbidden us from going without him. He and the boys have been so busy getting logs in for a corn crib that he hasn't had time to make the trip. Now you're sure it's no bother?* Alice quickly put her mind at ease and scooted closer to her brother as Celey approached the wagon.

After helping the girl aboard, Daniel climbed back up and steered the team toward Waldron. He wasn't listening to what the girls chatted about, but he noticed that Celey had a musical laugh and enjoyed the sound of her voice. A sharp pain in his ribs made him look at Alice, who said, *Daniel, Celey was speaking to you. Stop being rude.*

Daniel thought he saw the girl giggle as she glanced away. When she turned back, her dark eyes sparkled with mischief as she spoke. *Thank you again for your help the other day. I'm afraid I didn't properly express my gratitude. Father has been so busy trying to get the logs he needs from the forest that he's not had time to make the trip. I don't understand why Mr. Anderson would bother Amanda and me that way, but I was surely grateful when you stepped in.* Daniel nodded and said, *My pleasure.*

When they reached Waldron and Chamber's Mercantile, Alice and Celey quickly gathered the items on their lists. After seeing Caleb Reed mooning over a muzzleloader that Chambers had hanging on the wall, Daniel called Chambers over and gave him his list, deciding to provide Alice with a chance to visit with the young man. A group of men gathered near the cracker barrel, watching a spirited game of checkers; Daniel joined them.

He noticed as the girls made their way to where Caleb stood and saw his little sister 'accidentally' bump into him. He wondered where the little minx had learned to bat her eyes that way and at the pink flush on her cheeks as she apologized. Caleb looked like there was something stuck in his throat. He seemed to be trying to speak, but no words came out. Daniel saw Celey standing a bit apart, not intruding on Alice as she attempted to engage the young man in conversation. He watched his sister practice her feminine wiles on Caleb and listened with half an ear to the men talking about crops and working on the roads. Daniel didn't notice that Celey had stepped further away from the couple until he heard her scream.

Celey had wanted to give Alice some privacy, knowing that Alice was sweet-on Caleb and hoping he would notice her and ask to come courting. Celey looked at the yard goods, running her fingers over a length of blue linen. *Mother could make such a pretty dress for Amanda.* she thought. Out of nowhere, someone pulled her into the storeroom behind a stack of boxes. Celey smelled stale tobacco and what she imagined was corn liquor as a rough hand covered her mouth and a harsh voice whispered in her ear. *I told you that papa of your'n would be sorry if he didn't sell me that land. I reckon he needs a mite more convincin'; it's time for him to move on. I bet your kisses are mighty sweet. Be a good girl now, and stay quiet while I have a little taste.*

Celey was frozen in terror as she realized what Tom Anderson intended to do. He had her arms pinned and his hand over her mouth. She struggled, trying to get away, but he was too strong. When Anderson moved his hand to kiss her, Celey screamed as loudly as she could.

Chapter 6

One moment Anderson's foul breath had been burning her nose, and the next, she had heard a sound that reminded her of Papa's bull when her brother Jackson would tease it. After that, Anderson had flown backward into the boxes, and Celey somehow found herself in the wagon between Daniel and Alice.

Daniel stopped the horses when they got to the outskirts of town and asked Celey if she was hurt. She noticed his face was red with a thin white line around his mouth. She didn't recall seeing anyone so angry and was frightened because she had caused it. *Daniel, I'm so sorry that I...,* his look stopped her. *Celey, you have no reason to apologize. I owe you an apology for allowing that brute to touch you. If it's the last thing I do, he'll pay for putting his hands on you today.*

Back at the Dobbs farm, Celey - once again - reassured her Father and Mother that she wasn't hurt, only shaken up. They'd heard the story at least a dozen times, and each time she could feel the bile rise in her throat as she thought about Anderson's rough hands on her.

Caleb had insisted on following them back to the farm, fearing trouble from Anderson and his bunch. Now he and Alice were telling everyone again about hearing Celey scream and Daniel running across the store and *'walloping Anderson so hard that it broke his nose.'* Each time Caleb recounted what had happened, Daniel's *'bellow of rage'* was louder and his fist struck harder.

Levi had wanted to go after Anderson immediately. Being fourteen, he was prone to act before he thought. Caleb and Daniel laid hold of the boy before someone else got hurt. Harrison was going to see the Sheriff, and Daniel was going with him. He didn't trust Sheriff Ellis much further than he could throw the man. Daniel suspected Ellis of being in cahoots with Anderson. Mr. Dobbs was a good man, and Daniel respected him, but he didn't believe for a minute that the Sheriff would take care of Tom Anderson - at least not in the same way as Mr. Dobbs did. Daniel would feel better with his brother, Henry, nearby while they were in town, so he sent Levi to fetch him, giving the boy something to do.

When Henry arrived at the Dobbs' farm, Jefferson was with him. Daniel's pa was a peace-loving man, but Jefferson would not stand by while Tom Anderson mistreated his family and neighbors. Jefferson's first concern was for Celey and his daughter Alice.

Satisfied that Anderson hadn't harmed the girls, he turned to his son.

Daniel's hand had a clean cloth tied around the knuckles; some blood had seeped through and stained the white material. Jefferson could sense the anger his son was struggling to control. He knew that Daniel was feeling responsible for what had happened to the Dobbs girl; he also knew he needed to make his son see reason, or they would have a war on their hands - a war they were not yet prepared to fight.

Jefferson spoke in a rush, *Son, I see the murder in your eyes, and murder's what it would be if you go after Anderson now. I need you to use your head; I need you to hear what I'm saying. Henry and I will go to the Sheriff with Dobbs to ensure no harm comes to him. It would be best if you and Caleb stayed here in case Anderson or his bunch tries something while we're gone.*

Daniel felt torn. He wanted nothing more than to smash Anderson's face again. He knew Pa was right; if Daniel saw the man now, he might not stop hitting him. The memory of Celey's scream made his ears ring. He was angry that Anderson had violated her while <u>he</u> stood a few feet away.

He'd seen her looking at the yard goods and hadn't noticed anyone near her. Bird Jeter and Isaac Turpin were playing a lively checker match, and he'd gotten caught up in their rivalry. Her scream had made his blood run cold. Daniel didn't remember knocking over the checkerboard as he rushed to get to her. He didn't remember much of anything except the feel of Anderson's nose breaking under his fist. Daniel noticed specks of blood on his shirt and wondered if they were Anderson's or his own.

Harrison, Jefferson, and Henry headed into Waldron. Harrison wanted to kill the man who had dared lay hands on his Celey. In his present state of mind, he didn't believe that God would judge him too harshly if he did. The main problem with this was that Anderson always managed to wiggle out of whatever trouble he had. Harrison wasn't sure who all Tom had in his pocket but suspected the Sheriff to be among them. As the men rode along, they discussed what they feared to be true. Regardless of the accusations against Anderson, Fondren and Yates always provided him an alibi.

As they neared the edge of town, Jefferson signaled the men to stop. *I feel we should pray before we step into the lion's den.* He led them in a simple prayer, asking God to protect them and show them how to handle this situation.

Surprisingly enough, Anderson was in a cell when the men walked into the Sheriff's office.

Chapter 7

Tom Anderson knew he had made a mistake. He meant to force Dobbs to sell out, and part of that ploy had been Dobbs' daughter. Tom had thought to catch the girl alone, to scare her a bit – maybe steal a kiss. He had come from his still and been drinking too much when he'd seen her in the mercantile. Not thinking about the outcome, not looking to see who else was there, he grabbed the girl and pulled her into the storeroom.

She was a little thing, and keeping her still had been easy. Tom had reminded her of his earlier threat. He'd only meant to scare her; Anderson figured she'd run to her papa and beg him to sell. Dobbs – being yellow – would finally tuck-tail and run.

Tom shouldn't have tried to kiss her; not there. He should have waited. When the girl screamed, Tom gave her a little shake and warned her to keep quiet. After that, he remembered a crash and a blinding pain as Daniel Tilman's fist broke his nose. Tom owed that farmer; Tilman had interfered too many times now.

Chambers and the Sheriff had called him a fool; there had been too many nosy farmers in the store when Tilman hit him. The three had decided it was best to make it look like the Sheriff had arrested Tom. Sheriff Ellis would take Tom in; he would lay up in the cell for a few days, play cards with the Sheriff, and drink some whiskey. The farmers would be happy because Tom was in jail.

When Harrison Dobbs walked into the Sheriff's office with Henry and Jefferson Tilman, Tom was sitting on the bunk, still nursing his broken nose.

The door to his cell stood open, and before anyone realized his intent, Harrison had Tom pinned to the floor, beating the tar out of him. Ellis jumped up to stop the whipping and tripped over Henry's well-placed foot, allowing Dobbs to get in a few more licks before Jefferson pulled him away from Tom.

Henry helped the Sheriff to his feet; *Better watch your step there, Ellis; that could've been a nasty fall.* The Sheriff shot him an angry look before checking on his prisoner. Tom's broken nose was bleeding again, and his left eye was starting to swell. Any thoughts about Dobbs being a coward were long gone. Tom thought the man would kill him before Tilman pulled him away.

Ellis was yelling at Harrison, *Dobbs; you're under arrest! You can't bust into my jail and attack my prisoner that way!* Henry grabbed Dobbs' arm before he swung at the Sheriff, and things could get more out of hand; he guided the older man out the door. Henry knew his pa would be able to sort everything out. Jefferson wasn't one to start trouble, but he had a way of handling even the worst ruffians.

Jefferson turned to Sheriff Ellis and spoke in a firm voice. *Ellis, you won't be arresting Dobbs today. If you had done your job, none of this would have happened. The townfolk know you're in partnership with Tom and those two reprobates, Fondren and Yates. You all think you can take what you want without regard for the fella you're taking from. It stops now!*

Dobbs was defending his womenfolk; if Anderson had kept his hands off what don't belong to him, he wouldn't be bleedin' all over the place. The best thing you can do is keep him locked up for a few days and give heads time to cool.

You fellas think that because we're God-fearin' folks, we'll roll over or tuck-tail and run. You might want to spend some time readin' the Good Book; God was never a peaceful man, and his followers tend to be like him. As Jefferson stepped through the door, he turned and looked at Tom. *If anything happens to my boys or any of mine, you'll know the wrath of God firsthand.*

The men rode toward the Dobbs farm, each thinking about what had happened at the jail. Harrison felt no remorse for the thrashing he'd given Tom. He could not tolerate Anderson putting his hands on Celey. Harrison would repent but didn't have much hope that God would forgive something for which he wasn't sorry.

Jefferson chuckled. *Harrison, when I prayed for God to show us what to do, I thought it would be to keep our wits about us. Guess God told you Tom needed a good hidin'.*

At that, Dobbs laughed and felt a lightness in his heart. Maybe it had been the hand of God landin' those blows.

Back at the jail, Tom held a steak to his swollen eye and cursed the men who had battered his face. He had never expected Dobbs to be a fighter. The man was always 'turnin the other cheek' like it said in that Book of his. Tom had always been able to bully his way into getting whatever he wanted; no one ever stood up to him. Dobbs and Daniel Tilman were going to pay for what they'd done to him; they had to. Other folks would think they could stand up to Tom - if he let them get away with this. He had to get a handle on it and fast.

Tom and Ellis plotted their revenge. They would have to be careful; Tom's mistake with the girl had the farmers riled up. He'd lay low for a while, let them think he was scared of Dobbs. When they all felt safe, that's when he'd strike.

Chapter 8

Daniel's angry steps echoed as he paced across the porch at the Dobbs farm, unhappy to be left behind. He knew Pa was right; best, he stayed there considering his mood. Whenever Daniel thought about Anderson putting his hands on Celey, he felt murderous. Tom had terrorized the townfolk for too long, and today had been the last straw. Daniel was determined to end the wickedness that made it unsafe for his womenfolk to go to town.

As he continued his restless pursuit, Celey stepped out of the house. She noticed the furrowed brow and the hint of fury that surrounded him. She questioned whether she should disturb him and decided there might not be a better time. Softly she cleared her throat, the sound stopping Daniel's agitated pacing. Celey wasn't sure if the look he gave her was a grimace or a poorly disguised glare; she faltered when she spoke. *Daniel, I wanted to thank you for your earlier help and apologize; I understand that you're angry with me; I have no excuse for what happened, but...* Celey stuttered to a halt at the look on Daniel's face. She knew he was angry with her, but the outrage she saw there frightened her.

Breathing slowly, Daniel calmed himself, speaking so low that it forced Celey to step closer to understand his words; she cringed as he began to talk. *Angry at you! Oh, I'm plenty mad! Celey, how could you think that I'm angry at you? You've done nothing for which you should apologize. A woman should be able to look at yard goods without some scoundrel harassing her. I am the one who should be sorry. Anderson would never have gotten close enough to touch you if I hadn't been distracted by that fool checker game. I failed you; it's my responsibility to keep my womenfolk safe.*

Celey found that an odd thing for him to say. She wasn't his responsibility. She started to correct him when he interrupted her again. *Celey, I promise Anderson won't get near you again. I'll make sure of it.* She didn't understand why he was saying any of this. She was Father's responsibility, not Daniel's. He had no reason to apologize and no reason to look after her. Celey decided he must feel guilty and that it would pass given some time.

Not knowing what else to say, she thanked him and turned toward the door. That's when she noticed his hand. The white bandage was stained, deep red; Celey gasped and reached for his hand without thinking. She felt horrible. He was hurt, and it was all because of her. Still holding his hand, she led him to the kitchen and motioned toward a chair. Daniel sat and watched as she gathered a clean cloth, fresh water, and some ointment and placed them on the kitchen table. She quickly removed the bandage and shook her head when she saw the raw scrapes on his knuckles. She washed away the blood from his hand, patted it dry, applied the ointment then wrapped it with the clean cloth. Daniel watched as her dainty hands moved gently and swiftly across his larger one. He noticed how slim her fingers were and how soft her touch was. Daniel wondered why he was fascinated by them and why her touch felt so good. He also wondered when he'd begun to think of *her* as one of *his* womenfolk.

Daniel thought about taking her hand; he wanted to feel the softness in his rough one again. Just as he reached toward her, the door swung open, and his pa, Henry, Caleb, and Mr. Dobbs, came into the kitchen. Henry was already telling Caleb about the whipping Mr. Dobbs had given Tom Anderson. *Mr. Dobbs had old Tom pinned and was wearin' his fists out on him before we knew what was happening.* Daniel's eyes went to his pa's; Jefferson nodded and smiled. *Ellis was gonna stop him, but the clumsy man tripped and fell.* From the grin on Henry's face, Daniel wondered how much help Ellis had with that fall.

Clarissa, Amanda, and the boys, Levi and Jackson, joined Celey and the men in the kitchen as Henry recounted the trip for Daniel. Celey was shocked as Henry told them about her father beating Mr. Anderson. Everyone was muttering their approval and commenting that *He got what he deserved.* Celey felt sick; this was all her fault! She'd never heard of Father fighting. Two men she cared for had defended her in less than a day. She thought what a foolish girl she was to keep getting in Anderson's way. *Father, Daniel, I am very sorry I caused all of this.*

Harrison took Celey's face in his hands and said, *Daughter, you've done nothing wrong. It's I who should apologize. I thought this place would be better with time and wouldn't be so rough and wild. I know better; violence and wickedness don't stop on their own. Good men must take control and destroy them.*

Harrison then spoke to the men; *It's time we do more than sit by and watch while Anderson and his bunch run this town. It's time we bring some civilization to our home. I want my women folk to be safe even if I'm not beside them. We need to meet with the rest of the citizens and make a plan. We need a church.*

Clarissa served coffee and slices of cold biscuit puddin'. The group discussed what they needed to do to tame their wild town. They decided that Daniel, Henry, and Caleb would ride to the neighboring farms and talk to each family about meeting at the Dobbs farm the following Sunday. Levi was anxious to help, but Harrison feared the young man would find trouble if he rode alone in the countryside. He put Levi to building benches with the help of his younger brother Jackson. They thought to have a church service, Jefferson would read from the Bible, and they'd sing from Clarissa's hymn book. Everyone would bring dinner, and afterward, the adults would discuss the steps needed to make Waldron safe.

As the men made plans to take control of their town, Celey wondered when she had begun to care for Daniel.

Chapter 9

The week passed quietly enough. Everyone was busy with chores, and Caleb and the Tilman brothers made time to visit their neighbors. Word had spread throughout the county about Harrison Dobbs whipping Tom Anderson in jail. Each time someone repeated the story, it did a little more damage to Tom's reputation.

Folks were tired of Tom's bullying and sick of Sheriff Ellis not doing his job. They'd had enough of the high prices at the mercantile and not having regular fellowship with their neighbors. The turnout on Sunday promised to be sizeable. It appeared the actions of one man, brave enough to stand up for what was right, had given them the courage to change their little corner of the world. Each family had come to

Scott County looking for something better. They'd come because they heard what a good land it was. The land was good; the vermin that dwelled there were not.

Tom had gotten wind of what was happening; he and his associates needed to nip this nonsense in the bud. Chambers and Sheriff Ellis had made their way up the creek on his place, and the three sat around Tom's still, talking

about how to stop that bunch of meddling farmers from messing up their operations. Their scheme centered on the Dobbs and Tilmans. They were at the head of this nonsense to civilize Waldron. They'd underestimated Dobbs, but that wouldn't happen again. Anderson would have to be more careful; this time, he'd have to ensure he had an air-tight alibi. As Anderson considered his next move, he poked at the embers of the fire under his still. He'd have a good stream of Whiskey flowing in just a few more minutes.

Sunday dawned bright and warm; a gentle breeze stirred the trees. The day would be perfect for the meeting at the Dobbs farm. Daniel had been busy all week, too busy to stop by and check on Celey as he'd wanted to. He wasn't sure why he felt the urge to see for himself that she was safe. Dobbs wasn't about to let her go into town until things had changed, but Daniel needed to see her. He and Henry loaded the wagon and helped their ma and sister aboard. They were all looking forward to the day spent with neighbors and the chance to worship together. Daniel was anxious to develop a way to make their community more civilized; he wanted his women safe. Again he wondered why he included Celey as one of his own.

When the Tilmans reached Harrison's farm, wagons were already in the yard. It appeared that everyone was anxious to be together and to discuss their future. Henry helped his ma and Alice down, and the women made their way to where Levi and Jackson had set up makeshift tables. Alice glanced around, hoping to catch a glimpse of Caleb. The mood was light as neighbors greeted neighbors. Soon everyone was seated on the benches the boys had set under the trees, and Harrison stood to address his neighbors.

Folks, we appreciate everyone coming out this morning. It's good to see each of you. We'll start with Jefferson Tilman reading from the Lord's Book, and after prayer and a song or two, we'll enjoy our dinner. When the young ones get settled for a rest, the adults will discuss how we will change our town.

Jefferson had thought and prayed about what to say to the folks here and believed God had led him to this scripture. His voice was clear and robust as he read - *Matthew Chapter 18, verses 15-18:*

"Moreover if thy brother shall trespass against thee, go and tell him his fault between thee and him alone: if he shall hear thee, thou hast gained thy brother.

But if he will not hear thee, then take with thee one or two more, that in the mouth of two or three witnesses every word may be established.

And if he shall neglect to hear them, tell it unto the church: but if he neglect to hear the church, let him be unto thee as an heathen man and a publican.

Verily I say unto you, Whatsoever ye shall bind on earth shall be bound in heaven: and whatsoever ye shall loose on earth shall be loosed in heaven."

Jefferson had decided to wait until the afternoon to add his thoughts to the scripture. The group sang *A Mighty Fortress is Our God*;

"And though this world, with devils filled, should threaten to undo us, we will not fear, for God has willed his truth to triumph through us. The prince of darkness grim, we tremble not for him; his rage we can endure, for lo! His doom is sure; one little word shall fell him."

Jefferson led the group in prayer and blessed the food they were about to eat.

The women chatted as they filled plates for their men and children. Alice offered to fix a plate for Caleb so his mother could tend to her young ones. After they had served everyone, the ladies ate their dinner and kept an eye open for anyone who needed another helping of food.

The men's conversations turned to crops and stock; Isaiah Wood had a new bull. Samuel Riley was cutting logs to build a cabin; he'd been courting Nancy Kennedy and wanted to finish it before the preacher came around. The women visited about quilting and a better-than-usual crop of muscadines this season.

Celey sat a bit apart from the others - having found a stump that made the perfect table for her plate. She watched as Alice presented Caleb with a big slice of the apple cake she had baked and how her face lit up with a smile when Caleb asked her to join him. She listened with half an ear to the conversations taking place around her. Everyone enjoyed the food and the rare opportunity to fellowship with their neighbors. As Celey ate her dinner, she pondered the words Mr. Tilman had read and frowned. There had been so much talk of violence of late. She supposed it was sometimes necessary, but she wished folks could be kind and get along. Celey didn't notice Daniel watching her from the shade of a pine tree.

Daniel was curious about what caused the little furrow between Celey's brow. He wanted to smooth it away. As soon as that thought crossed his mind, he shook his head; *What's the matter with me? She's just a girl.* Still, he thought about that 'girl' at the oddest times. Daniel needed to protect her. He didn't understand why he felt that way. Maybe it was because of what had happened at the mercantile. He was still angry that he hadn't noticed

Anderson hanging around. It made Daniel sick to think of Tom touching one of <u>his</u> women.

The meal ended with many compliments to the women folk and girls who had prepared such a bounty. Everyone grew quiet as Jefferson Tilman stepped to the front of the group.

Chapter 10

Neighbors who know me also know that I'm a peaceful man. The Lord tells us to turn the other cheek, but there comes a day when it's time not for peace but vengeance. The Book also tells us that when we're trespassed against, we're to go to that person, and if they don't change their ways, we're to think of them as a heathen and bind them.

No one among us hasn't had dealings with Tom Anderson. The man makes it his business to sow fear and evilness. I believe you have all heard about Anderson putting his hands on Dobbs' oldest girl, Celey. My son Daniel has 'gone to him' as the Lord tells us to do on two occasions. After the second one, Harrison, my son, Henry, and I went to him again. I don't *believe the man is of a mind to change his ways. We all know that he and the Sheriff are in it together, so we can't count on help from the law.*

I came to Scott County some seven years ago. I heard this was a grand land and wanted a part of it. I've been wrong in waiting for others to make it a more civilized place. It's high time we all get together and stand to make our town safe for our women and children. The crowd murmured their agreement, and a few 'Amens' came from the group. No one had noticed the solitary figure crouched in the shadows.

Other men from the gathering spoke, and soon there was a plan to build a church. Everyone agreed that the place to start with change was in the Lord's house. They decided each family would donate logs from their timberland, and Jasper Reed would oversee the log count. Those families that didn't have timber would help by snaking logs to the mill to have them cut into boards. Jasper had also volunteered to donate an acre of land; his place was almost in the middle of everyone. Abraham Fisher had heard about an itinerant preacher in the next county; some families planned to attend his services. Hopefully, by the time they finished building the church, they'd also have a preacher to lead them in worship.

There were some suggestions of ways to deal with Tom and his associates, but without having a Sheriff they could depend on, they weren't sure how much they could do.

The decision to build the church had caused a stir of excitement. The ladies were already talking about having a community dinner each month. Everyone felt lighthearted as the women uncovered the cakes and pies left from dinner and set out steaming pots of coffee and pitchers of cold milk. Conversations buzzed as small groups shared their little community's plans for the future. Celey overheard one such conversation that left her feeling uneasy.

A woman Celey didn't recognize was saying to Mrs. Reed; *It's so lovely that Celey has Daniel to look after her. It must be a comfort to Clarissa to know her girl has such a fine man to care for her in the future.*

Why on earth would the woman think that she was Daniel's responsibility? Celey kept telling him and everyone else that she wasn't. It was true that he had rescued her twice now, but that was just his way of being a good neighbor. Celey was agitated; she frowned as she tried to reason out how to stop folks from thinking Daniel was looking out for her.

Daniel didn't know what was causing that look of irritation on Celey's face, but he knew he wanted to make it go away; he wanted to hear her laugh. Daniel had enjoyed the way her eyes danced and the sound of her laugh on the day she rode with him and Alice to town. He wanted her to smile; Celey was too pretty to have that crease between her brows. Daniel wasn't sure why, but he needed to protect her and ensure she never frowned again.

Daniel and Celey would have been shocked at the number of conversations folks had about them that day. It seemed that the only ones who didn't know that they were in love were the 'happy couple.'

Chapter 11

Work on the new church moved swiftly. The congregation spent every moment they could spare cutting timber, stacking, and preparing the logs. The acre that Reed had donated was mainly clear of trees, so they could start building as soon as they had enough material. There was always someone at the site working.

Jasper sent word to his neighbors when all the timber had been cut into boards, sorted, and stacked. They would meet on Saturday and begin work. Anticipation was thick as women discussed what they would bring for the dinner that they would have, and the men gathered their tools.

As the Tilman wagon reached the Dobbs' farm, Alice asked if she could ride the rest of the way with Celey.

Sitting with Celey in the back of the wagon, Alice began to whisper about Caleb. *He asked Pa if he could call on me, and Pa agreed. I haven't seen much of him, with him working every spare minute at the mill on the logs for the church. Whenever Daniel or Henry snake logs in to cut, I beg to ride along. Caleb is always so happy to see me. I hope we'll be the first to marry in the new church. It would be exciting, but Nancy Kennedy and Samuel Riley might beat us.* Celey was smiling and nodding; Alice was talking so fast that she barely breathed between her sentences. Celey's mind was wandering when she heard Alice hiss. *Celey, you aren't paying attention to me at all!* Celey apologized and asked her to repeat what she'd said. Alice answered; *I said that you'd understand how wonderful love is when Daniel asks your father for permission to call on you.*

Whatever she might have thought Alice would say, this was not it. The girl had lost her mind. Daniel, call on <u>her</u>! Whyever, would his sister say such a thing?

Daniel was riding his horse behind the wagons; he needed to ensure nothing happened to his girls. When Celey suddenly looked up from whispering with his sister, her face was flushed, and her eyes flashed. Daniel smiled and tipped his hat. Somehow Celey managed a somewhat crooked smile and a slight nod.

Alice must be mistaken; why would Daniel wish to call on her? That was absurd. Because Alice was in love, she thought everyone that spoke to one another was too. As Alice continued to prattle about Caleb and how wonderous he was, Celey tried to devise a way to avoid Daniel. She mustn't be rude, but she had to stay far away from him.

People had the wrong idea, and Celey must stop their gossip now. She hadn't realized the wagon had stopped until Daniel stood before her, offering to help her dismount. Celey was inclined to ignore him and scramble down the best she could, but that would not be polite, and Mother had raised her better.

Celey allowed Daniel to help her from the wagon, and after a hastily muttered *Thank you*, she bolted to find her mother. Clarissa and the other ladies were busy brewing coffee and preparing to fix hoecakes and sidemeat for a mid-morning meal. Celey busied herself with mixing batter and prayed she'd be able to avoid Daniel the rest of the day.

The men and older boys had a well-designed system to build as quickly as possible. As the men brought the boards to the site, Jasper and Caleb had them make four stacks, one for each wall. The Reeds had set the foundation stones. A team of men gathered at each pile and framed the four walls. By mid-morning, the men had finished the framework, and boards were quickly being nailed into place to cover the frame.

When the men took a short break, Celey served coffee from a large kettle, carefully pouring the hot liquid into the cups the men held before her. She was concentrating on not spilling when Daniel spoke; she splashed coffee over his hand. As she apologized, she mentally scolded herself for her clumsiness and drawing attention. Daniel returned to work, thinking about how pretty she looked when she got flustered.

Work stopped for the noon meal after the men had finished the walls and cut openings for windows and the door. After dinner, they would build the trusses and start covering the roof. Some of the older boys would start building benches for pews. They arranged for someone to go to Little Rock for window glass and a bell. Everyone agreed that there must be a bell. Spirits were high as the folks admired the men's work so far. There was talk of church socials, and they all wondered how soon they could find a regular preacher.

Bird Jeter suggested that Jefferson Tilman and Isaiah Wood could read the scriptures until the preacher came the next month. Everyone agreed; they were all anxious to have a place to worship together.

Celey managed to avoid Daniel during the meal by helping the little ones. He had seen her across the way, talking to the children and fixing their plates. Daniel noticed how patient she was and how softly she spoke to them as she ensured they had napkins tied around their necks and weren't eating with their hands. Occasionally he heard her soft laugh as one of the children said or did something that amused her. The sound drew him to her.

Celey was comforting a fussy baby and didn't notice Daniel until he spoke. *You sure have a way with these little ones.* She was so startled it was a wonder that she didn't drop the poor child. She wished he had a bell tied around his neck so she would know he was there. She was beginning to look like she had some affliction, always jumping and spilling things when he was around. Celey smiled, unsure what to say, and continued to rock the baby. She had no idea how appealing she looked at that moment. When she didn't respond, Daniel nodded and went back to work.

By late afternoon, the church had a roof. There was still much to do, but they were well on their way to having their church. Everyone was excited and agreed to hold their first service tomorrow since the weather was so mild. As wagons pulled away and neighbors went to their chores, they called to one another, *See you in church tomorrow.* Their hearts were full of joy.

Chapter 12

The fire was blazing through the church when Jasper Reed smelled the smoke. He and Caleb fought it as best they could, but they could have done nothing to save the building.

As the families arrived the following day, tears began to flow. All the excitement and hard work from the past weeks were gone. Jasper, Caleb, and Abraham Fisher were still pouring buckets of water on spots that smoldered, their faces covered in soot and their eyes rimmed red. There was a constant hum of voices as folks discussed what could have happened. A few among them were bolder and made accusations against Tom Anderson, causing the crowd to murmur in agreement. When The Dobbs and Tilmans arrived, the group was ready to ride into town and string Anderson up.

Jefferson Tilman stepped up on a stump and quieted the din of angry voices. *Neighbors, I'm not saying that you're wrong; I'm not saying that whoever did this shouldn't be punished. I'm saying that we, as Christians, must be careful in how we handle this. We're no better than that scoundrel if we rush into town and hang a man without first making sure he was the one who did this.*

Let's pray that God will grant us wisdom and that, with His help, those responsible will be dealt with justly. Jefferson had a way about him that made folks listen to him, and the mood shifted from revenge to justice.

After praying together, the men sifted through the rubble, hoping to find evidence to support their suspicions. Daniel pushed a board with the toe of his boot. The movement caused the smoldering embers to reignite as air reached them. Daniel poured water from the bucket he carried on the tiny flame, and that's when he saw it. There in the ash lay a piece of Tom Anderson's pipe stem. There was no mistaking whose it was. Tom smoked a pipe he'd gotten in a trade with the Indians. The long stem was carved from bone and had figures cut into it. Daniel called over the other men. He wanted witnesses to see it before he picked it up.

The congregation decided that Jefferson, Harrison Dobbs, Jasper Reed, Abraham Fisher, and Daniel would ride into town to confront the Sheriff about the fire at the church. Sheriff Ellis was even less helpful than they expected, but he said he'd look into it. As tempted as they were to deal with the situation, they knew it would be best to let the law handle it. The men decided to send Caleb and Henry to Fort Smith for the United States Marshall; they agreed to keep this quiet and to keep an eye on Anderson and Sheriff Ellis until the men returned with the Marshall.

When the delegation returned to the church site, they found the rest of the congregation had been busy. They had watered down any spots that still burned and had begun sifting through the rubble. They had managed to salvage some of the benches; the rest was beyond repair. The talk had already turned to cutting more timber and starting again. They had decided to change their town and wouldn't let this tragedy stop them. They realized the church was just a building, a place to gather and worship. The true church was in their hearts; no fire could take that from them. They'd rebuild and continue their strategy to make Waldron safe.

Tom lay low, deep in the timber at the back of his place. Gus Yates had brought out supplies earlier. He'd told Tom that those infernal farmers were stacking more wood to rebuild the church. Tom had been sure that if the blame thing burned down, they'd give up on their fool notion of civilizing <u>his</u> town.

Gus and Fondren hadn't been able to get close to the rubble. There was always someone there keeping watch with a gun. Tom was apprehensive about this; he would have felt better if they'd been able to poke around. He'd been careless again, broken his pipe stem, and needed to figure out where he had been when it happened. It wasn't a big piece, but it was big enough that most folks would know it was his.

After Gus left, Tom tried to remember where he had been when he'd broken the stem. He recalled spending most of the day at his still, The farmers had been building that confounded church, and he'd needed a quiet place to figure out how he'd stop them. He'd sat there, sippin' Whiskey and plotting how to get back at Daniel Tilman and Harrison Dobbs in particular.

About dark, he'd made his way to Jasper Reed's place. He'd watched from the trees as the folks had left for home, callin' out how'd they see one another in church the next day. Tom had waited until the lights went out in Reed's cabin, and then he'd slipped into their church; he was surprised at how much they had done. That just made it all the better for him. Burning it down now would be almost as good as if they had finished it.

Tom had stumbled around the dark building; his day spent with his whiskey jug had left him unsteady. He'd been looking for something to use as fuel, hoping someone had left one of those camphene lamps or even a lard burner. Tom had struck a match to help him see and tripped over something. He remembered landing hard and the crash as his whiskey jug broke. The next thing Tom knew, the place was on fire. Not exactly how he planned it, but as long as the church burned, he'd be okay with it.

Tom had tasted blood on his lip and realized that when he fell, his pipe had been in his mouth; he must have landed on his face. Tom had scrambled around in the light from the fire, looking for his pipe, and found it a few feet away. He'd meant to gather up the broken jug, but the flames were spreading too fast. Tom had known Reed would be there soon and didn't want to get caught.

He'd stood in the trees, watching Reed and his boy fight the fire. Tom had been almost giddy as they raced to their well and back, knowing they would never be able to stop it. He'd wanted to stay and watch the rest of the church folk arrive. Seeing their dream go up in smoke made him feel better about his broken nose. Tom had slipped further into the woods, not realizing he'd left his mark at the scene of his crime.

Chapter 13

The week was a busy one. Not to be defeated, the congregation had worked harder than before, cutting timber and taking the logs to the mill. The stacks of rough-cut lumber quickly grew, as did excitement for the day they would be able to rebuild their church. The men took turns standing guard at the site with no hint of trouble. No one had seen Tom Anderson since before the fire.

Henry and Caleb returned to Waldron, accompanied by the United States Marshall. Marshall Hensley wasted no time investigating the fire scene; afterward, he headed into town to see what he could uncover.

Before they left Fort Smith, Hensley had spoken to Elias Crenshaw about his barn burning. Crenshaw had told him about Anderson pressuring him to sell his property and that his barn had burned when he refused to make a deal. Sheriff Ellis said a lantern had caused the fire, but Crenshaw swore he had not left a lantern in the barn. Henry Tilman had told the Marshall about Anderson trying to buy his pa's place and the Dobbs' place. He'd also told him about the Dobbs girl's run-ins with Anderson. Hensley had to admit he'd have liked to be a fly on the wall when her pa tore into Anderson at the jail.

He knew that Sheriff Ellis wasn't the most ethical man. Many frontier towns lacked men of good moral character as leaders. Hensley was sure that Ellis was working with Anderson and Chambers.

Chamber's Mercantile had a reputation for shady deals, and Marshall Hensley had reports of Chambers selling stolen merchandise. He'd heard about Chambers and his little arrangement with Tom Anderson. Hensley had also heard about Gus Yates and Laben Fondren vouching for him whenever Anderson was a suspect in something underhanded. Something was crooked here; he needed proof, though. He was determined to find the truth of what had happened at the church, and he wanted to investigate a few other things.

Hensley was sure that Chambers had turned a sickly shade of green when he walked into the mercantile. The Marshall identified himself and stated that he had questions about stolen goods and needed to see Bills of Lading for any shipments Chambers had purchased in the past six months. Chambers started to balk, but Hensley cut him off; *That wasn't a suggestion.* As Chambers hurried to do as ordered, the Marshall noticed a man slip from the store. *Good thing I brought along my Deputy.*, he thought.

Laben eased out of the mercantile and headed out of town. He needed to let Tom know about the Marshall at Chambers' store. Those lousy farmers had gone and made a mess of things for them. He'd liked it better before all those do-gooders started showin' up. They had a good thing going, Chambers, Yates, Tom, and him. They had put aside a pretty good sum of money, and once they got rid of Tilman and Dobbs and had access to that spring, they'd make a heap more.

They would have to go easy for a while; the Marshall wasn't like Sheriff Ellis. Ellis could see the advantage in a bit of dishonesty. They all needed to keep to their story and ride this out. When that Marshall left, they would turn up the heat on old Tilman and Harrison Dobbs; then they would hightail it out of there as Crenshaw had. Lost in his thoughts, Laben never noticed the man following him through the timber.

Sheriff Ellis walked into Chambers' Mercantile just as Chambers handed the shipping papers to Marshall Hensley. He quickly tried to introduce himself and assure the Marshall of his full cooperation. Hensley raised a hand to silence him as he compared Chambers' paperwork against a list of stolen merchandise. The Marshall noticed each time there was a stolen shipment in Ozark; Chambers had received an identical shipment within a week. Hensley tucked the papers into his book and left Chambers and Sheriff Ellis staring after him.

Next, Hensley went to Tom Anderson's freight office. He didn't expect to find Anderson there, but that might work to his advantage. When the Marshall asked to see the freight logs, the young man behind the counter was naive enough to think nothing was amiss. Hensley sat at Tom's desk, looked over the entries, added the pages to his collection, and noticed the stem of a broken pipe peeking out from under a stack of papers. He then headed out to Crenshaw's old farm.

No one had bothered to clean up the mess from the fire. Hensley had taken Elias Crenshaw for a mild-mannered man, not one to put up much of a fight. Crenshaw had packed up his family and moved them to Fort Smith in record time. Hensley knew finding anything was unlikely, but he always needed to see things firsthand.

The barn was severely damaged but not beyond repair. The Marshall found a broken lantern in the corner of a stall, a peg to hang it on, nowhere nearby. Looking around the barn, Hensley noticed that the pegs for the lanterns were all shaped like a crook, meaning the lantern couldn't accidentally slip off the peg. While he couldn't say for sure, he suspected someone had deliberately broken that lantern in the stall.

Hensley then rode to Jefferson Tillman's farm. Henry had done an excellent job filling him in on everything that had happened, but the Marshall wanted to talk to Tilman and his son Daniel. He felt that he and his Deputy might need some help before settling everything, and the Tilmans sounded just about right for the job.

Jefferson Tilman was a good man. He was just and fair. It was evident to Marshall Hensley that while he wouldn't start trouble, he'd never stand by and let someone hurt his family or a neighbor. Daniel offered to show the Marshall around their property when the conversation turned to Anderson trying to buy them out.

The men made their way through the timber and finally to the spring that fed the creek, which ran through Tilman's,

Dobbs', and Anderson's property. Hensley was sure that spring was behind Anderson's desire to own that land. He knew Anderson was a moonshiner, and while that wasn't illegal, right now, there was a lot of noise being made to outlaw the untaxed production of distilled alcohol again. The most critical ingredient in moonshine or any other liquor was water. That spring water would make a fine product. If distilled alcohol did become illegal again, the backwoods still operators would make a lot of money.

When Marshall Hensley headed to the Dobbs' farm, Daniel Tilman insisted on going with him. Hensley got the impression that Daniel had taken a personal interest in what had happened to the Dobbs girl. He'd just met Daniel, but he already pitied Anderson if he ever bothered that girl again.

Harrison Dobbs was as different from Jefferson Tillman as the day was from the night. Yet, it was easy to see that Dobbs would not stand by while anyone molested his family. Again, the Marshall wished he could have seen the incident at the jail. Dobbs answered all of Hensley's questions calmly and very matter-of-factly. When Hensley asked to speak with Celey, he watched as Daniel Tilman positioned himself like an archangel ready for battle. *Yes, the man was quite smitten with the girl.*

Celey was quiet in her answers, and the Marshall noticed that she shifted the blame for her encounters with Anderson to herself. He also saw the scowl on Tilman's face deepen each time she did. Hensley asked Celey to repeat Anderson's threat several times, and she never varied the wording. '*You tell that papa of your'n that he better sell me that land, or he's gonna be right sorry.'* He marveled that neither Dobbs nor Tilman had beaten the man to death.

Marshall Hensley thanked them for their time and rode off to meet his Deputy. He was anxious to hear what he'd turned up, and they needed to make arrangements.

Daniel knew he should head home, but he hadn't seen Celey in several days, and being near her, he felt less apprehensive. He was glad when she offered him a cup of coffee and some cold biscuit puddin'; if he took his time eating, he might be able to wrangle an invitation to supper. The thought made him shake his head. *What was he doing? She was just a girl.* Still, he couldn't shake the feeling that she was his responsibility and that he needed to protect her.

Chapter 14

Deputy Jeremiah Hanes had followed Laben Fondren from the mercantile and up through the timber to a still site. The wind was calm, and the smell of woodsmoke and sour corn mash cooking had not been detectible until they were almost at the site. Hanes had stayed far back in the trees and listened as the men had talked.

Fondren was telling two other men about Marshall Hensley looking around at the church and questioning Chambers about his shipments. Jeremiah heard one of the men utter a curse, and Fondren said, *Tom, we never counted on the U. S. Marshall sticking his nose in this. What's he likely to find now that he's poking around?* A voice, Hanes suspected to be Tom, answered, *Those blame farmers are causing me nothing but trouble. If that Marshall looks too close, he'll figure out those stolen shipments ended up at Chambers and that I'm the one that shipped them. You need to find that piece to my pipe stem before one of those goody two shoes finds it. We're all going to be in a mess if that happens.*

Hanes wanted to rush in and arrest the men, but he knew that three against one was poor odds. He slipped quietly away through the trees and met up with Marshall Hensley to compare the information they had found.

Marshall Hensley was waiting at the church. The men decided to make their camp there and hopefully avoid further vandalism. Hanes filled the Marshall in on what he'd seen and heard at the still site. They went over Chambers' shipments and Anderson's freight logs. Hensley found it interesting that Chambers' purchases were identical to the stolen goods from Ozark, but

Anderson's freight logs showed they came from Fort Smith. The Marshall sent Hanes in to send a telegram to the depot in Fort Smith. Hanes was to be sure that anyone nearby heard that he was inquiring about the shipments Anderson brought in. When Hanes sent the telegram, he was to go back to the freight office and question the man working for Anderson. The Deputy would then stop by the jail and talk to Sheriff Ellis about the fires at Crenshaw's and the church. Marshall Hensley was hoping that by the two of them questioning each person repeatedly, someone would get nervous and slip up.

Hensley wandered the town, talking to people at random. Sometimes the person you least expected had the answers you needed. He found that the opinion around Waldron was that Anderson and Chambers were in cahoots and were running prices up;

since there wasn't another store, folks had no choice but to pay them. Several men were vocal about Tom Anderson and his association with Fondren and Yates; a few even mentioned what they thought were dirty dealings between Sheriff Ellis and the men. Hensley had the impression that Harrison Dobbs whipping Anderson at the jail had turned the tide against Anderson. It was funny how it only seemed to take one man standing up for what was right to cause others to find the courage to do the same.

Marshall Hensley had a lot of information that pointed to Tom Anderson and his associates; the problem was there were no eyewitnesses. He and Hanes went over everything again and, after talking to the delegation from the church, announced that they didn't have enough evidence to make any arrests. They told the men to let them know if anything else happened, and they'd be happy to investigate.

It didn't take long for word to reach Tom that the Marshall had returned to Fort Smith. He immediately began thinking about how to rid Waldron of that church and the Tilmans and Dobbs. Fondren told him the farmers were going to rebuild this Saturday. He knew everyone would be at Reed's working on the church, and he would have the perfect opportunity.

Saturday dawned warm and sunny. The group that gathered to rebuild the church was considerably more than before. After word of the fire and the altercation between Harrison Dobbs and Tom Anderson spread, more folks decided it was time for a change in their community. As wagons arrived, Jasper Reed organized the men into four groups and set the older boys straight to building benches. The women set up their makeshift kitchen, started pots of coffee, and made preparations for a mid-morning meal. The older girls were in charge of the younger children, keeping them from underfoot and caring for the babies. Everyone had a job, and the excitement crackled in the air.

Jasper's system had worked well before; now that it was familiar, the men had the frame up in no time. Before they stopped for coffee, the men were already nailing up the slabs of lumber that covered the walls. No one tarried over their break, anxious to get back to work. The plan was the same as before; if they got the roof on, they'd have service the next day in their new church. Tonight, some of the men would stand guard. No one wanted a repeat of the fire.

A few miles away, glass shattered as a burning torch crashed through Jefferson Tilman's cabin window. At that exact moment, a shot rang out as

Jeremiah Hanes threw a bucket of water on the flames. Down the road at Harrison Dobbs' farm, Marshall Hensley stood over Tom Anderson's lifeless body. Anderson wasn't dead, which was surprising. Daniel Tilman was a hard-fisted man. Anderson had just drawn back to throw his torch when Tilman came down across the back of his neck with both fists; Anderson fell like a tree. Hensley had kicked dirt over the torch before anything could catch fire. Tilman tied Tom up, and they tossed him in the back of the wagon. They'd heard the shot from Tilman's farm and were anxious to get there.

When they arrived at Daniel's home, they saw the broken window and Henry pulling a half-burnt curtain from it. He nodded in the direction of the barn where Hanes stood. One man was tied up, and a blanket covered another man's lifeless body.

Yates had managed to throw his torch through the window. As Hanes moved to throw water on the flame, Fondren had stepped from the barn's shadow; his rifle pointed in Hanes' direction. If Henry hadn't seen Fondren, Hanes would be under that blanket. They loaded the men in the wagon with Anderson and headed to the Sheriffs.

Sheriff Ellis never expected to see that group pull up to his office. They all thought the Marshall had gone back to Fort Smith. He knew Tom was preparing to put more pressure on the farmers, but he never imagined it would end up this way. The Sheriff didn't know if Tom was alive or dead and suspected that it was Fondren under the blanket. Ellis knew he needed to be very careful. Everything they had worked for was unraveling before their eyes. Ellis ignored the Tilman brothers and spoke directly to Marshall Hensley.

Marshall, I didn't know you were still in the area; it looks like you ran into a bit of trouble. Marshall Hensley ignored the Sheriff and said something to Henry Tilman, who rode away toward the County Judge's house. Hensley turned to Ellis then. *Sheriff, I'll be using your jail for my prisoners, and I'll want you to fetch Chambers.* Ellis opened his mouth to protest. How dare the man give him orders in <u>his</u> jail? The look on Hensley's face made the words catch in his throat.

By the time Ellis returned with Chambers, the Judge had arrived, and Tom had come to himself. Elam Burrel, the County Coroner, was talking to Henry and Deputy Hanes. Judge Collins was seated behind Sheriff Ellis' desk. Ellis noticed Jefferson Tilman and Harrison Dobbs standing off to the side. Whatever was happening here wasn't good for him or any of the men he had associated with for years. The Sheriff began concocting a story in his mind to clear himself of anything they blamed on him. At that moment, it was every man for himself, and he wasn't willing to take a fall for anyone.

Judge Collins nodded to the Marshall to begin. As it turned out, Mashall Hensley had been working with the Sheriff in Ozark, trying to find whoever was stealing shipments of dry goods. They had located a man who sang like a bird when he was facing jail time. The man told them about his arrangement with some drivers. He would "hold them up and knock them unconscious" when they woke up, he would be gone with the wagon, and they would have a shiny five-dollar gold piece.

The problem was that he had robbed the same drivers over and over. When the freight master caught on to his scheme, the man gave up Tom

Anderson as the mastermind behind it and Fondren and Yates as the men driving the wagons away from the 'hold-up.' Marshall Hensley had been able to tie Tom to the freight; the Bills of Lading from Chambers' had been the final nail in his coffin.

Hensley then explained what he knew of the fire at the church. The men had found pieces of a broken whiskey jug in the rubble, nearby was a piece of a pipestem. It appeared that whoever set the fire had either broken the jar intentionally or had dropped it. The pipe stem could indicate that someone had been smoking a pipe and either dropped it or used it to start the fire. The broken piece, though small, was very distinctive and fit perfectly into the stem of a pipe the Marshall had found at Tom Anderson's freight office.

Hensley then addressed the events of the day. When Deputy Hanes had followed Laben Fondren up to Tom's still site, he'd overheard Tom and his cronies discussing intent to burn the new church and the Dobbs and Tilman cabins. He'd heard Tom talking about finishing what he started with the Dobbs girl. Hensley and Hanes made a show of leaving Waldron, saying they didn't have enough evidence to arrest anyone. They had circled back to the Tilman farm, and the Marshall had deputized Daniel and Henry Tilman. Henry had waited there with Deputy Hanes; Daniel had accompanied Hensley to the Dobbs' farm.

Deputy Hanes had been inside the Tilman's cabin when the torch shattered the window. Henry saw Fondren step from the shadow of the barn, rifle aimed at Hanes. He'd called out for him to drop the gun, but Fondren turned on Henry, and Henry shot him. Yates had tried to run, but Hanes had reached him before he made the timberline.

At the Dobbs' farm, a similar scene had played out. Tom wasn't as fast as Fondren, but he may have been luckier. Before Tom managed to throw his torch, Daniel had knocked him out.

Chambers was the first to crack. *I don't know why I'm here. I've done nothing but buy goods for my store. How was I to know they'd been stolen? Everything I bought from Anderson was in good faith.* Tom Anderson lunged at Chambers, cursing him as a traitor. Judge Collins' fist came down on the desk; *Chambers, you need to sit down and keep quiet. Anderson, you'll control your tongue and your temper!*

The Judge listened as each person told their version of the events from the past several weeks. He barely concealed his anger when Daniel Tilman spoke of Tom Anderson's abuse of the Dobbs girl. When Sheriff Ellis told about Harrison Dobbs whipping Tom in the jail cell, Collins fought back a smile of satisfaction. When everyone had said their piece, Judge Collins was quiet for a time as he mulled over each man's story.

After hearing from each of you today, I believe that Tom Anderson and Asa Chambers have been robbing this town blind for long enough. Chambers jumped to his feet, but the Marshall pressed him back into his chair. *The time for good men to take this town in hand has come. By their admission, Anderson, Fondren, and Yates conspired to burn the church and the homes of Harrison Dobbs and Jefferson Tilman. From the testimony of Marshall Hensley and Deputy Hanes, they have been working with the Sheriff in Ozark, who has in custody a man who has identified Anderson, Yates, and Fondren as stealing loads of freight. Anderson has, on two occasions, threatened and physically abused Miss Dobbs. A piece from Anderson's pipe was found at the fire scene when the church was burned, along with a broken whiskey jug. The only alibi any of you have is each other, and considering the events of today, I would say that won't hold up in a court of law. Ellis, you've stayed quiet through all of this. My guess is you're trying to figure out a way to wiggle free of your bad decisions. Ellis, as Sheriff, you were entrusted with keeping this town safe. Instead, you threw in with the ones from which the townfolk needed protection.*

Marshall Hensley, you and Deputy Hanes will take Mr. Chambers, Tom Anderson, Gus Yates, and Sheriff Ellis to Little Rock to await trial for multiple charges, including arson and attempted murder of your Deputy.

The accused men lunged at each other, screaming their innocence and threats for revenge. Judge Collins continued, *I'm assuming that Mr. Tilman and Mr. Dobbs will be making a complaint against Anderson and Yates for attempted arson. Until an election, I'm appointing Jefferson Tilman as Sheriff. I believe that's all for today. Marshall Hensley, I want to visit the new church; kindly remove these prisoners.*

Chapter 15

The first service in their new church was a time of celebration. Judge Collins and many of the families from the town joined them in their worship. News of the arrests of Tom Anderson, Asa Chambers, Gus Yates, and Sheriff Ellis had spread like wildfire bringing a sense of freedom and safety that the folks had never before experienced.

After worship and singing, Harrison Dobbs led the congregation in prayer. He asked God to expose all the evil the men did and for justice for their actions. Many were surprised when he continued the prayer by asking God to bring them to repentance and help them find their way to Him.

The congregation spent the afternoon enjoying delicious food and conversing with friends and neighbors.

Everyone wished the day would never end, but there were cows to milk at home, and morning chores came early. Alice rode in the back of the Dobbs' wagon, whispering with Celey. Daniel would guide his horse close to them now and then, hoping to hear Celey's laugh.

Daniel dismounted at the Dobbs' farm to help Alice from the back of the wagon. He knew she didn't need help, but he wanted an excuse to be near Celey. Daniel offered his hand to help her dismount, and she took it shyly. Her hand was as soft as he remembered from the day she'd bandaged his. He tipped his hat and said, *You look mighty pretty today, Celey.* Her dark eyes flew to his, and the faintest blush colored her cheeks; she stuttered a quiet, *Thank you.,* and hurried to the house. Daniel smiled as he climbed back on his horse; he wasn't sure but thought her pretty brown eyes were peeking through the curtain as he rode away.

Marshall Hensley sent word of a trial date for Anderson and his crew. Daniel, Henry, Jefferson Tilman, Harrison Dobbs, Caleb Reed, Elias Crenshaw, and others would need to travel to Little Rock to give testimony. The Judge had also requested Celey testify; Daniel had exploded over this news. He would not allow her to be humiliated on the witness stand. Anderson would never have the opportunity to leer at her and scare her again. Judge Collins sent a letter to the Judge in Little Rock explaining that the Tilmans and Caleb Reed could testify to the events involving Miss Dobbs and asked that she not be required to testify.

The Waldron delegation met Marshall Hensley and Deputy Hanes on the day of the trial at the Courthouse. Hensley informed them that Yates, Ellis, and Chambers had been 'singing like canaries.' The Judge had sentenced Ellis and Chambers to two years in the Little Rock prison; he'd given Yates five years. Today they would only need to testify against Tom Anderson. Hensley told them the Judge was ready to throw the book at Tom.

Each man took his place on the witness stand and told of his experiences with Anderson. The Judge mused how he'd like to have seen the whipping Harrison Dobbs gave the man. When Daniel Tilman took the stand, the Judge wondered how Anderson was alive to stand trial. The contempt and tightly controlled rage that Tilman felt seeped from him as he told about Anderson accosting the Dobbs girl. The Judge thought Anderson was one lucky man to have walked away with only a broken nose.

After hearing the testimony of the men from Waldron, Marshall Hensley, Deputy Hanes, and the statements from

Anderson's accomplices, the Judge told Tom to rise. *Tom Anderson, after weighing the testimony given in this courtroom and the statements of your former colleagues, I find you guilty on all counts. I hereby sentence you to life at hard labor in the Arkansas State Penitentiary.*

As a guard led Anderson away, he cursed the men and screamed threats of revenge for what they had done to him.

Back in Waldron, the citizens actively took a hand in changing their town. After her husband's arrest, Mrs. Chambers sold the mercantile and moved back to Missouri. Tom Anderson's wife put a For Sale sign on the Freight Office and Livery door. For a while, folks were abuzz about Mrs. Anderson coming to town. No one could remember the last time they had seen her. Everyone knew Tom had a wife and children, but they never came down from the mountain.

Work continued on the church; the steeple was finished and ready for the bell. Jasper Reed set the glass panes in the window frames. The congregation was excited because the circuit preacher would come the next month to hold his first service in the new church. Afterward, there would be dinner, and the preacher would marry Samuel Riley and Nancy Kennedy.

Alice wouldn't be the first bride in the new church, but her time would come soon enough. Caleb had asked permission to marry her; Jefferson had reluctantly agreed. It wasn't that he didn't like the young man; it was just that Alice was so young. Alsey reminded him that she had been fourteen when they married, and Alice would be almost seventeen by the time Caleb finished their cabin.

Alsey had been married in a beautiful lace dress that belonged to her grandmother; she and Alice were making it over for Alice to wear at her wedding. Alice was sewing or doing needlework items for her hope chest every moment she wasn't working on the dress. Celey, caught up in Alice's excitement, was making Alice a sampler with her and Caleb's names.

Each time they were together, Alice said something to Celey about Daniel calling on her. The first few times, Celey ignored her and quickly changed the subject to Alice's wedding. After a few times, Celey began to wonder why Daniel hadn't come to call and if he ever would.

With Tom Anderson and the others behind bars, the women of Waldron felt safe going to the mercantile without their menfolk. It was a heady freedom for Celey and Amanda to take the wagon to town and shop for Mother. Jefferson Tilman had appointed Bird Jeter Deputy. Bird lived in town, and it was easier for him to keep an eye on the town. Things had been mighty quiet, the only excitement being the checker game they had moved to the Sheriff's office, so Bird was handy if anyone needed the law.

As they drove past the Sherriff's office, Celey noticed Daniel leaning against a post, watching the game. The men were laughing and joking, enjoying a respite from their work. When they entered the mercantile, Celey gave their list to Mrs. McCollister. The McCollisters had moved to Waldron from Ozark and purchased the store. Mr. McCollister was a short, balding man with rosy cheeks and sparkling blue eyes. He was always friendly and made Celey feel comfortable in his store. His wife was a tall, thin woman. She wore her dark hair pulled back into a tight bun; the severeness of her hairstyle accented her high cheekbones. Celey thought she was attractive, but she was slightly intimidated by her.

It was lovely to take her time and look at the yard goods and whatever else caught her eye. Mrs. McCollister had rearranged the store, and light came through the clean windows. She had the displays attractively arranged, and Celey knew if she allowed herself, she could spend hours looking at all the pretty things for sale. She turned toward the counter and ran smack into Daniel's broad chest. Her heart gave a strange little flutter as he grasped her arm to steady her.

I'm sorry I haven't been by to see you, Henry and I bought our farm from Pa, and we've been a might busy. Absentmindedly he tucked a curl behind her ear. Celey's cheeks grew warm when he said; *I'd forgotten how dark your eyes are.*

Celey thought he was acting very strange. His following words caught her off guard. *I stopped by and asked your father for permission to call on you. He's given it, but you should have the final say. Celey, may I call on you?*

Chapter 16

Celey wasn't sure whether to laugh or cry. Daniel Tilman had asked for permission to call on her. Her heart soared in her chest as she spoke softly. *Yes, Daniel, I'd be honored if you called on me.* She was sure her feet weren't touching the ground at that moment. She was trying to commit the moment to memory, knowing that she'd want to revisit it once she was alone.

Daniel watched as a dozen emotions played across her pretty face and wondered about each one, unsure why he felt so nervous. Daniel knew that if she'd said no, he'd have found a hole and crawled into it. Celey was waiting for him to say something else, but he just wanted to look into her big dark eyes. Finally, he found his voice and asked if she'd like to go on a picnic on

Saturday; he had something to show her.

After Daniel left the store, Celey wandered to the counter in a daze. She didn't even hear Amanda asking her about what Daniel Tilman had wanted. The ride home was quiet. Amanda soon abandoned trying to talk to her. Celey was so lost in her thoughts that she never heard her sister say, *Jeesh! I think I'll pass if that's what love does to you.*

Alice stopped by a few days later. Celey wasn't sure which of them was more excited about Daniel asking to call on her. *Oh, Celey, we'll be real sisters now!* The girls discussed Alice's wedding plans and the picnic Daniel was going to take Celey on. He'd sent word with Alice that his ma was packing a lunch for them, and he'd be by for her about 10 a.m. Soon it was time for Alice to go; she had lots of sewing to do.

The remainder of the week passed quietly. Each day Celey would wake and realize that she had a suitor, and each day, she would panic. What did he want to show her? What if they had nothing about which to talk? What if he found her boring? On and on her list of worries went. She would have been surprised to know that Daniel was doing the same thing, only he was saying all these things to his brother, Henry.

Henry found it amusing at first that his big brother was so nervous. She was just a girl, after all. By the end of the second day of listening to all his misgivings and fears, Henry was ready to hold Daniel's head underwater for a bit.

The
brothers
were cutting
trees with a
cross saw;
once again,
Daniel had
stopped to
express his
concerns -

Finally, Henry said, *Daniel, if you don't hurry up and marry that girl, I swear I will punch you whenever you open your mouth. It's as clear as the nose on your face to everyone except the two of you that you're crazy about each other. Now stop driving me crazy and get busy on your end of this saw.* Daniel started to say something else, then hesitated. He was pretty certain Henry was joking about punching him but being brothers, you could never tell for sure.

Saturday morning, Daniel was up earlier than usual. He had done his chores and was brushing down his horse, Barnaby. Henry came out to the barn, rubbing sleep from his eyes. He watched as his brother ran the brush over the horse until its coat shone like a copper penny. Henry wondered if a girl would ever make him act that way.

Daniel arrived at the Dobbs' farm precisely at 10 a.m. He spent a few minutes talking with Mr. Dobbs in the yard before the man called for Celey. She stepped out of the house, and Daniel knew he'd never seen anything as pretty as she was. She wore her long, dark hair pulled back at her neck, and her dark blue dress made her eyes look like midnight. Daniel wondered when he'd started to think like a poet.

They'd ridden a ways in silence, each struggling to think of something to say that would be interesting. When they passed Daniel's home, Celey asked where they were going. Daniel would only tell her he wanted to show her something special. Quiet again, they were content with their thoughts until Daniel pulled off the road and began to make his way up what appeared to be a freshly cut trail.

They hadn't gone far when they came to a small clearing. Celey could hear a creek running close by and noticed that the trees appeared to have been recently cut. Daniel pulled the wagon into the shade of a large pine and then helped Celey down from the wagon seat. He took her hand and led her to the center of the clearing. Celey thought what a pretty spot it was and how a cabin would be perfect just there in the shade of that big pine.

Daniel had rehearsed what he wanted to say at least a thousand times. He was sure the chickens and cows could have said it for him; they'd heard it many times. Daniel placed his hands gently on Celey's shoulders and began the longest speech of his life.

Celey, I love you. I'm not sure when that happened, but I know I do. I want to spend the rest of my life with you. This little patch of land doesn't look like much yet, but I can have a cabin built in no time if it suits you. There's water right close, and we wouldn't be too far from your folks. Celey, we could have a good life here. I promise to protect you and keep you safe. I promise to love you always. I'd be honored if you'd agree to marry me.

Tears welled in her eyes as Celey threw her arms around the man she loved.

Hand in hand, they walked to the creek, and Daniel promised to take her up to the spring that fed it one day. They forgot about their picnic, caught up in the wonder of building a home and life together. Daniel agreed that the spot under the pine would be perfect for their cabin - he'd hoped she would pick it. They decided where to put a garden and the barn and shyly talked of the family they would one day have.

Daniel told her that Henry and his father had agreed to help him get the cabin built. He'd been cutting logs and hauling them to the mill.

Caleb and a few other men said they'd help using the same system they had done at the church; Daniel was sure they could have a cabin dried-in in about a day. They hoped to marry when the preacher came the next month but agreed not to tell anyone. They didn't want to take away from Samuel and Nancy's celebration.

When they thought of the picnic Alsey had packed for them, it was time for Daniel to take Celey home. They'd spent their day daydreaming about their future and learning about each other. Celey learned that Daniel couldn't carry a tune in a bucket but could whistle. He didn't like hoecakes but did like sourdough pancakes. Celey revealed that she was scared of frogs, but she loved to go fishing with her brothers.

Daniel told her about how he and Henry had intended to start their farm and about Henry telling him that he'd gladly wait awhile to build his cabin as long as he didn't have to listen to Daniel mooning over Celey. That made Celey blush and her heart flutter, knowing he had been thinking of her. She protested a bit about Henry having to wait on his cabin, but Daniel assured her that Henry had been the one to suggest this arrangement.

As Daniel lifted her into the wagon, he gently brushed her lips with his and sighed; *Mrs. Daniel Tilman.*

Chapter 17

The following two weeks passed in a flurry of activity. The bell for the church arrived from Little Rock. Jasper Reed and Abraham Fisher mounted it in the church's steeple. Everyone agreed they wouldn't ring it until the first time the preacher came.

Nancy Kennedy had everything except herself moved into her new home and anxiously awaited the day she would become Mrs. Samuel Riley.

Every moment they could spare, Daniel and Henry worked on the cabin. Their pa, Jasper and Caleb, helped as often as they could. Celey tried to work on items for her hope chest without raising suspicion. Clarissa thought she had gotten caught up in the excitement of Nancy and Alice's upcoming weddings. She hadn't seen Daniel as often as she would have liked but knowing he was building their future home helped soothe the nerves strung so tight Celey was sure they would break.

Saturday before the preacher came, Daniel stopped by and asked if Celey would like to take a ride. They headed in the direction of their future home. Celey was shocked when they pulled into the clearing, and a pretty little cabin stood under the big pine tree.

Happy tears streamed down her cheeks as she realized she would marry the man beside her tomorrow.

Celey didn't sleep much that night. She tried to lay still and close her eyes, willing herself to fall asleep, but sleep eluded her grasp. She lay in the bed next to her sister and thought of how her life would change after tomorrow. Tonight was the last night Celey would spend under her father's roof, the last night she'd share this bed with Amanda. Tomorrow she would have her own house and be responsible for the meals and laundry. Celey laid out her garden in her mind trying to remember which seeds to plant for a winter garden. Tomorrow she would go from Mother and Father's daughter to Daniel's wife.

Celey thought about how surprised Alice would be. Alice was sure she would be the second bride in the new church. Celey had asked Daniel if they could be married outside, not wanting to take that from Alice. She hoped her new sister would be happy for her.

Then she thought about Amanda; she was going to be mad at Celey for not sharing her secret. She loved Amanda wholeheartedly, but the girl could never keep a secret.

As the sun rose over the horizon, Celey's eyes began drooping. Amanda shook her sister, saying, *Wake up, sleepy-head. Today's the big day!* Celey's eyes flew open. Did Amanda know her secret? Amanda continued, *The first service with the new preacher and then the dinner and wedding. Celey, why are you so tired? You look like you haven't slept a wink.*

Celey made her way through her chores without thinking. After helping Mother clear the breakfast dishes, she went to her room and tried to undo the damage of a sleepless night. She'd drawn a fresh pitcher of cold water from the well and sat with a cool, damp cloth pressed to her eyes. Celey prayed the cold water would make them less puffy and erase the dark circles. Thankfully Amanda had already dressed, and she and Mother were packing their dinner baskets. Celey brushed her hair until it glistened and pulled it back with a dark blue ribbon. She dressed in her Sunday clothes and made sure her boots were shiny. When she'd done all she could to make herself presentable, she walked out to the wagon that would take her to her destiny.

Daniel had tossed and turned almost all night. At one point, Henry threw his boot at him and told him to sleep or at least be still. He'd nearly spent the night at the cabin but realized this would be the last night he spent in his parent's home. He thought about his ma and pa and the Christian example they had always been for him and his siblings. Pa always put God first in his life and had always protected his wife and children. Ma had raised them to respect their pa and to love each other, but the most important thing she taught them was to love God. Daniel lay in his bed and prayed that he would be a good husband and provider for Celey and the children he hoped they would have someday. When sleep finally claimed him, he was at peace with his future.

When their wagon pulled into the churchyard, Celey began to search the crowd for Daniel. She saw him across the way, deep in conversation with Caleb. Before she could make her way to him, the bell began to ring, and everyone found their way inside for the first service with the new preacher.

Reverend Logan greeted the congregation and thanked them for asking him to be their pastor. He complimented them on the fine job they had done on the church building and explained that, for now, he would be visiting them once a month. Jefferson Tilman and Isaiah Wood would share the responsibility of holding services in his absence.

The Reverend spoke from the book of 2 Chronicles 7, verse 14 – *If my people, which are called by my name, shall humble themselves, and pray, and seek my face, and turn from their wicked ways, then will I hear from heaven, and will forgive their sin, and heal their land.*

He spoke about how the people had come together and built this fine church, but they understood that the true church was in their hearts, not this building. He talked about how they had stood up for righteousness and taken their town back from the sins of the Devil. He encouraged them to continue to pray and seek the will of God and said that God would indeed bless this little gathering.

After his closing prayer, he reminded them that when they'd

finished their noon meal, they were all invited to attend the wedding of Miss Nancy Kennedy and Mr. Samuel Riley.

Celey joined her family on the blanket her mother had spread for their picnic. Around them was a steady hum of voices as folks talked about the service and the wedding to follow this afternoon. She looked around for Daniel, hoping to see him walking toward her. She finally noticed him standing with the Reverend; the men seemed intent on their conversation.

Reverend Logan had listened as Daniel had explained his request. He understood young people's eagerness to marry when they had access to a minister, but he felt he would be remiss if he didn't also speak to the other parties involved. The Reverend promised discretion and made his way toward the Dobbs family. After introducing himself to Clarissa and the children, he addressed himself to Celey.

I hear that you'll require my services one day soon. Celey met his eyes with a bashful smile and nodded. Clarissa spoke up and told the preacher how thankful they were that God had blessed their girl with a man like Daniel. The Reverend exchanged a few more pleasantries and then made his way to visit with the next family.

When they packed away the leftovers and settled the small children on the blankets in the shade, the rest of the congregation filed back into their church to celebrate the first of what they hoped were many marriages.

Nancy and Samuel stood before their family and neighbors and vowed to love, honor, and cherish each other. They pledged their love to each other before God and their congregation. When Reverend Logan presented them as husband and wife, the gathering cheered.

Everyone spoke to the happy couple, offering their love and congratulations. Before the group could leave, Reverend Logan called for their attention. *My dear friends, today is a day of rejoicing. Please join me in celebrating the rites of matrimony between two more of our young couples.* The crowd erupted in gasps and whispers.

Celey and Alice stood next to each other, wondering who else could be getting married that day. As they pondered this, Daniel and Caleb walked toward them. The girls squealed with delight as they realized they were having a double wedding.

At the end of a long and joy-filled day, three young couples rode toward their new homes, excited about their futures.

Chapter 18

Celey and Daniel settled into their life together. What they lacked in things, they made up for in love and imagination. Daniel and Henry got their first crop in, as the three of them agreed to go forward with that part of the original idea for the brother's future. Henry was often at the cabin, helping Daniel build the barn or Celey with her winter garden.

Alice and Caleb stopped by whenever they visited the Tilman farm. The young women laughed about how they'd ended up having a double wedding and their husband's ability to keep a secret. The men had worked tirelessly to finish both cabins, neither hinting why they needed the help. The girls were truly sisters now, and they loved spending time together. Alice had not worn her ma's dress but had packed it away for her daughter to wear someday.

Alice was helping Celey make curtains for the widows Daniel had put in the East wall of the cabin. Celey could prepare their meals  and look out over the forest at the back of their home. She loved the woods. There were so many things to see. She was fascinated by the smells of the pine needles and the texture of the bark and cones. She loved the pretty patterns the sunlight made as it filtered down through the trees.

Celey couldn't imagine any place in the world where she would rather live.

Their life was simple. They quickly fell into a pattern, church on Sunday and dinner afterward with one of their families. Her mother and Daniel's ma had given Celey some chickens, and Daniel had built a pen for them. Each morning, Celey would gather eggs while Daniel milked their cow. She fixed their breakfast, and then Daniel worked in their field, cut timber, or did an odd job in town. Celey worked each day on making their cabin into their home.

As Christmas approached, the newlyweds made plans to spend the day with family. Christmas Eve was on Sunday, and they would all assemble at the church for a time of worship and celebration of the birth of Christ. Afterward, the Dobbs and Tilman families would gather at Harrison and Clarissa's; Celey was excited about her first Christmas as a married woman.

Christmas Eve dawned cold and crisp; light snow had fallen during the night. Celey was in awe of the beauty of God's handiwork. The pine boughs covered in snow and frost reminded her of the finest lace. She had warmed quilts in front of the fireplace and prepared pocket yams to help keep them warm. Daniel brought the wagon around, bundled Celey in, and they set off for church.

Reverend Logan read to the congregation from Luke Chapter 2. Celey had always loved the story of the birth of Jesus. As the Reverend spoke, she thought of Mary and how she had traveled to Bethlehem to give birth in a stable. Celey pondered, as Mary had done, and silently prayed that God would help her to raise her children to follow Him. At the end of the service, they sang *Silent Night* before everyone went to their homes.

At the Dobbs' farm, the mood was festive. Clarissa had placed pine boughs above the doors, and the scent was heavenly. A turkey roasted in the oven, and the smell of freshly baked pies and cakes filled the air.

The family reminisced about Christmases past, each sharing their favorite memories. They talked of the changes the year had brought to their community. Briefly, they spoke of Tom Anderson's family. No one had seen Mrs. Anderson since she put the for sale sign on the livery. Everyone wondered how she was getting along. Some men from the church had ridden up to her place with supplies, but she turned them back, saying, "I want nothing from those who took Tom from my children." They didn't linger on the bad but focused on all the good that had taken place. They talked of the new church, the Reverend, and the new family members now that the Tilmans and Dobbs were more than neighbors. They spoke of the unexpected weddings and the church socials. Each of them shared something for which they were thankful. Alice was grateful to have a sister, at last. Harrison was thankful his Celey had such a fine, Godly man to care for her. Jefferson read the passage from Luke to them again, and they talked about what it must have been like for Mary and Joseph so many years ago. They sang *Angels from the Realms of Glory*, *Hark the Herald Angels Sing*, *Joy to the World,* and *The First Noel.*

Levi kept the fireplace burning, and everyone was warm and toasty. Each time someone mentioned heading for home, another story or song started. Before they realized it, it was after midnight, and they agreed everyone would stay at the Dobbs' cabin. Celey and Alice would sleep with Amanda, Alsey would share Clarissa's bed, and the men could bunk on the floor near the fireplace.

Daniel offered his hand to Celey to help her stand from where she had been sitting on the rug. As she placed her hand into his, he felt something strange in his palm. Daniel stared a moment at the tiny, knitted socks in his hand. As realization dawned on him, he let out a whoop and pulled Celey into his arms, swinging her around in circles. Of all the gifts he could have received, Celey's was the most precious gift of all; he was going to be a Pa!

Chapter 19

Daniel asked Celey for the hundredth time if she was sure she was having a baby as he helped her from the wagon. Celey laughed and tousled his hair as he gently set her on her feet. When they stepped inside their cabin, Celey was surprised to see a rocking chair sitting near their fireplace. Daniel had managed to slip it inside before they left the day before. His ma enjoyed rocking while doing her needlework and mending. He'd thought Celey might enjoy the rocker; deep down, he had hoped that soon there would be another reason for her to use it. Little had he known that his timing was perfect when they'd headed to church on Christmas Eve.

Winter was a busy time for the Tilmans. Celey was sewing

nightgowns and knitting socks and caps for their baby. Alice stopped by one warm afternoon to bring Celey the prettiest little quilt she'd ever seen. Alice had made it, especially for her niece or nephew. She also had news to share. Alice and Caleb were going to be parents this year. She and her ma figured she should deliver in late Summer when Celey and Daniel's baby was about two months old. The women talked about how wonderful it would be to have children so close in age and dreamed about the cousins playing together and how they hoped that by the time they were old enough, there would be a real school in Waldron.

The first hint of Spring made Celey's heart sing. Daniel had forbidden her to gather the eggs during the winter. He was concerned she'd slip on the ice and injure herself or their child. She understood his concern and appreciated not having to bundle up and go out into the cold each morning, but she was starting to have cabin fever. Henry had taken over her garden, and while it was exciting to see the produce he would bring inside, she longed to dig her fingers into the dirt. The trips to church on Sunday and to the folks afterward had become her way of marking time. Daniel moved her rocking chair onto the porch so she could safely watch the world shake off its winter mantel and see the budding of Spring.

The sun shining across her face awakened Celey. As she stretched her muscles, she thought about how lazy she'd gotten since Daniel had taken over gathering the eggs. Since she didn't have to get dressed to go out into the cold, she slept a bit later in the morning. Celey found her slippers and robe and headed to the kitchen to start breakfast. As she walked from their bedroom, Daniel called out, *Happy Birthday!*

Oh my, she thought, I'm seventeen years old today. Daniel kissed her cheek and led her to a chair. He'd prepared their breakfast and in front of her was a tall stack of sourdough pancakes. Daniel was always saying she should eat more now that she was eating for two, but honestly, that stack was big enough for an army. She hoped Henry would come by in time to finish them off.

Henry did come by in plenty of time to share their breakfast. He dropped a small package into her lap and a kiss on the top of her head, saying, *Happy Birthday, little sister!* Celey carefully untied the string and unfolded the brown paper, taking time to smooth the creases and set it aside for reuse. Tucked inside was a book of Nursery Rhymes. She'd never seen such a wonder. Mother had told them rhymes when they were children, but that had been from memory. In her hands was the most beautiful little book with color illustrations of the verses and stories Mother had told them. *Oh, Henry, it's lovely!* Henry just smiled.

Henry wasn't the only one with a present for her. Daniel came through the door carrying something rather large covered with one of her quilts. He placed it in front of Celey and made her close her eyes. When he told her to open them, she burst into tears. The most beautiful cradle she had ever seen sat before her. All the months that Daniel wouldn't let her go to the barn, he'd been working on it. It was even more special to her because his pa had helped him with the intricate carving.

That evening they rode over to Jefferson and Alsey's for a birthday celebration. The entire family was there; as soon as Celey saw Jefferson Tilman, she burst into tears. Oh, Pa, thank you so much! The crib is beautiful. Jefferson wiped a tear from his eye. He'd come to love his new daughter and was anxious to meet his first grandchild.

With the winter behind them, Celey returned to her garden. Daniel had taken her to town for seeds, and their mothers had shared some from their past harvests. Henry had turned the soil, and he and Daniel helped her put in radishes, lettuce, collards, squash, cucumbers, sweet corn, Irish potatoes, and purple hull peas. Daniel had tried to discourage her from planting so much, fearing with the new baby, she would be overwhelmed. Henry had told him he'd come by each week and make sure she didn't do too much; he'd always enjoyed helping their ma in her garden.

The first crop of wheat the brothers had planted was coming on nicely, and they were sure to have a good harvest. They would cut their wheat in late May if the weather held. Daniel had been cutting timber and milling them into lumber to build a room for the baby. Celey told him their little one wouldn't need a room for a long time, but his excitement drove him on.

Late in May, Daniel and Henry harvested their first crop. The brothers were thrilled with their success. After setting aside their seed wheat, they sold the remaining grain for $420.00. Henry was anxious to start work on his cabin; he'd met a young lady whose family had moved to Waldron from Little Rock.

Caleb and Daniel helped Henry as often as they could. Levi would come every chance he had to help; he enjoyed spending time with his brothers and knew that the day would come when he would need their help to build a cabin. Today he had brought Celey two new chickens. Mother had more hens than they could use and sent Alice and Celey each two. Levi couldn't get used to his sister being a Ma. He liked the idea of being an uncle; if she had a boy baby - he'd teach it to fish.

Henry wasn't in quite the hurry Daniel had been to finish his cabin. He knew he'd have to court his girl a mite longer than Daniel had Celey. The Beck family had only been in Waldron since Christmas, and Mr. Beck was bound to know him better before agreeing that he could call on Elenore.

Celey's time of confinement drew closer. Daniel noticed that as she moved around the cabin, she pressed a hand to her back. He'd asked Levi to stay with them so he could fetch Clarissa when Celey's time came. When Daniel came in from the barn and found her doubled over, her knuckles white from clenching the edge of the table, he sent Levi for her mother.

Sarah Jane Tilman was born in the wee hours of the morning on the sixteenth day of June 1844. Her Pa fell head over heels in love with the little girl.

Celey teased Daniel that he would spoil Jane to the point that no one would ever want to marry her. Daniel was secretly agreeable with that; sure, there would never be a man worthy of his little girl. Jane was a happy baby who rarely cried.   If her Daddy wasn't holding her, she was content to lie in her cradle while Celey did her chores. On the rare occasions that Jane did cry, it made the hair stand up on the back of Celey's neck. When Jane had a touch of colic, Daniel insisted on holding her until she fell asleep.

When Jane was two months old, Alice gave birth to her son, Jasper Jefferson Reed. Caleb teased that the boy would never learn to spell that mouthful of a name and nicknamed him Jazz.   The name stuck, to Alice's dismay, and before long, she gave up correcting people and began to call him Jazz herself.

Chapter 20

Henry completed his cabin and barn. He and Daniel had a second crop in, and Mr. Beck had agreed to allow Henry to court Elenore. The new babies were healthy and happy, and the family gatherings revolved around who got to hold them. Surprisingly, Jane had stolen Levi's heart as she'd stolen Daniel's. Jane would coo and wave her chubby little arms whenever she heard Levi's voice. Daniel had confided to Celey that he couldn't have been happier than to know his baby girl had an uncle that loved her so. He said it made it easier to live with the thought of something happening to him, knowing that Levi would care for her as his own. When Daniel would talk that way, Celey would scold him. They had a long life ahead of them, and she didn't want to think about anything ever happening to separate them.

As Christmas again drew near, the family was preparing for another wedding. Henry and Elenore would wed in January. Celey liked Elenore and looked forward to having another sister nearby.

Celey had sewn a dolly for Jane's Christmas gift, and Daniel had cut wooden blocks and painted them with numbers and letters. They knew she was too small to play with the toys, but it gave them great pleasure to think of the first Christmas morning with their baby girl. Celey thought of Mary and the gifts Jesus had received that first Christmas long ago. She understood how much they must have meant to the young mother.

Christmas day dawned mild and bright. Unlike the year before, there was no need to bundle in quilts. They pulled into the churchyard just as Harrison and Clarissa arrived. Celey was worried about her mother. Clarissa assured her she was fine, but the woman who had always been full of energy seemed tired. After everyone had kissed Jane and exclaimed how much she'd grown, the family made their way inside.

Reverend Logan greeted them this fine morning with the news that he would be moving to their little community in the Spring. He would still travel one week each month, but they would have their preacher close by the rest of the time. Finally, having a preacher was another blessing among the many they had experienced in the past two years.

As Reverend Logan read the account of the birth of Jesus, Celey again thought of the young girl, Mary, alone except for Joseph, so very far from home and family. She whispered a prayer of thanks that her Mother and Ma Tilman were so near.

This year the family gathered at Jefferson and Alsey's. The Becks joined in the festivities. Mr. Beck was reserved at; first, but before long, he told Elenore he expected her to make him a Grandpapa straightaway as he bounced Jazz on his knee.

After a fine roast turkey and yams meal, the family gathered around the fireplace to share why they were thankful. Everyone was grateful for the babies, Jane and Jazz. Henry was thankful for the crop they'd gotten in and for Mr. Beck allowing him to marry Elenore. Amanda was grateful that she wouldn't have to share her bed with Celey and Alice this year.

As Celey listened to each person express gratitude, she remembered the year before. She was thankful that God had sent Daniel Tilman as her guardian angel. When Mrs. Anderson crossed Celey's mind, she said a silent prayer for the woman. She couldn't imagine how difficult it was for her to raise a family without her husband.

Clarissa was sitting in a rocker near the fire, the soft light from the flames played across her serene face and  the face of the sleeping baby girl she cradled in her arms. Celey wished she could draw; she would love to capture the moment of pure love between her little girl, Jane, and her Mother, Clarissa. She closed her eyes and committed the scene to memory; it was one that she would think of many times in the days ahead.

The new year came in like a lion. A blizzard dropped two feet of snow across the county. Henry was sure that they would have to delay his wedding. He'd moved into the cabin with Celey and Daniel on the second day of the storm. It was easier for them to keep one place warm than two, and Henry and Daniel took turns caring for the livestock they'd brought into Daniel's barn. Celey couldn't remember being as cold as she had been the first day or two. After the snow began to pile up against the cabin walls, it felt warmer. They all slept near the fireplace and spent hours talking about their childhoods and the ambitions they had for the future. Celey loved hearing the brothers laugh about when they were boys and the tricks they would play on each other. Daniel had once talked Henry into rubbing soot on their legs so they wouldn't have to wear socks in the summer. Everything had been fine until they had gotten the black on Ma's freshly washed sheets that night. They remembered the whipping Pa had given them; his heart hadn't been in it as he struggled not to laugh at their antics. Thankful they had gotten away with their prank, they had decided socks might be safer to wear than soot.

Ten days into the month, the storm broke. The sun peeked through the clouds, and the weak light began to warm the earth. Three days before the wedding, the only obstacle they faced was mud. Daniel was uneasy about Celey and the baby making the trip to the church. He worried that they might get stuck in the mire, and if the weather were to turn off bad, it could be deadly.

Henry finally told them the only thing to do was for him to ride to town on horseback. He figured he could take his time, and he would make it just fine.

Henry reckoned he'd stop at his parents and Celey's folks and tell them it might be best if they stayed home. After the weather cleared and the ground dried, the family could gather for a celebration. If the mud was too deep, he and Elenore would stay in town for a few days before coming home to their cabin. Though they hated to miss the wedding, it only made sense to stay home; if they got stuck on the road, who would look after the stock? They certainly didn't want to risk being caught in the cold with Jane.

Henry and Elenore returned home five days later. Henry recounted the trip to town as they sat at the supper table with Celey and Daniel. *The first mile wasn't too tricky. I guided Old Buster through the muck, and there were plenty of patches of frozen vegetation for him to walk on. We stopped at Pa's and warmed up; I cleaned the mud from Buster's feet and let him rest for a while. Ma didn't want me to continue. She said I'd make Elenore a widow before I made her a wife or some such silliness.*

The stretch of road between Pa's and Celey's folks was more of a challenge. The snow hadn't melted much, and there was right-smart ice underneath. Buster did real good, but I could tell it was winding him. It took us better'n four hours to get there. When we finally got to Celey's folks, Levi took old Buster into the barn and gave him a good rubdown and some feed. Mr. Dobbs insisted I stay there for the night; honestly, I was too tired to argue.

The next morning, I headed out again. Me and Buster made it to Caleb and Alice's in a fair amount of time. We stopped there so I could clean the mud off Buster's feet and warm up a bit. Thankfully there hadn't been too many wagons on the road, and we made it to town by evening. I was sure glad to get to the livery and settle Old Buster in a stall.

I wish you coulda seen Elenore's face when she opened the door. She busted out cryin', threw her arms around my neck, and gave me a big ole kiss right in front of her Pa.

Elenore gently chided Henry; *You don't have to tell everything you know, dear.* The smile on her face told her side of the story. She was happier than she'd ever been. Her Pa had told her a thousand times not to worry, but she just knew that Henry wouldn't make it and they'd have to wait until next month, when Reverend Logan returned, to get married.

Chapter 21

The remainder of the winter was mild. Light snow fell a few times, but nothing compared to the blizzard in January. Jane was fascinated by the snowflakes. Daniel would bundle her up so that only her eyes peeked out. He would catch the snowflakes and present them to her. She tried to wiggle free of her wrappings each time, wanting to touch the " *pretty*" that her Pa held before it went away. After a great deal of struggling, Jane freed one tiny hand, and when Daniel held the snowflake close, her finger touched the frozen bit of lace. Her little mouth formed a perfect 'o' as she said, *Ooooo cold!*

Celey and Elenore decided to have a garden together. Henry had plowed a spot for Celey the year before near the creek. The young women chatted excitedly about what to plant. They would start with beets, cabbage, carrots, onions, and peas. They would add beans, sweet corn, and Summer squash the following month. There were berries along the creek, and Daniel had discovered a PawPaw tree near the spring.

Jane was growing like a weed and would soon be one year old. Celey would read to her from the book her 'Unca Henny' had given her, and she tried her best to recite her favorite rhyme, *Pat-a-cake*. While she couldn't say the words very well, she could 'pat the cake.' Daniel declared her to be the most brilliant little girl ever born.

Celey had made several trips to visit her mother. Clarissa reassured Celey that she was well. She had been so tired because she was with child. Jackson, her youngest, was eleven; Clarissa never dreamed she would ever have another baby. Celey worried about their mother and spoke to Amanda and the boys about helping her around the house. Celey knew that Mother had lost three babies, and her heart had broken each time. She couldn't imagine what she would do if anything happened to Jane. Each time her mother crossed her mind, Celey would pray that God would protect her and the life she carried inside her body.

Jane was starting to pull up and trying to take her first steps. Daniel and Celey couldn't believe she was almost a year old. When her little legs would grow tired of trying to walk, Jane would drop to her knees, and it was all Celey could do to catch the little girl. She was too fast!

Elenore and Celey's vegetables flourished. The women tended their garden daily. Henry had plowed an area near the creek the first year, and he and Daniel built a wooden trough that ran from the water to their garden. The

men had carefully plowed between the rows of plants building the dirt up into berms. When the garden needed water, all the women had to do was raise a small door at the end of the trough, and a stream of water would pour from the creek into the rows. The women thought their husbands were the most resourceful men in the world.

Jane loved playing in the dirt and creek while her ma and aunt pulled weeds or dug vegetables. Celey would pin a piece of twine to Jane's dress and her own. As fast as the little girl was, she wasn't taking any chances of her getting in the creek if she were distracted.

While picking berries along the creek bank one afternoon, Elenore confided to Celey that she was expecting her first child. She hadn't even told Henry. Elenore told Celey she was frightened. She was an only child, and Jane was the only little one she'd ever been around. *What if I drop it?* Elenor exclaimed. *Oh, Celey, how will I ever know what to do?*

Celey hugged her new sister and assured her she would be a wonderful mother. She also reminded her that she and Daniel were just a stone's throw away if she needed help. Celey knew Henry would be so happy. He adored Jane and Jazz and was anxious to be a papa. Sunday at church, Mr. Beck told everyone who would listen that he would be a Grandpapa. Daniel chuckled. *You'd think he was the one expecting a child.*

Clarissa hadn't come to the service. Father had said she was just a bit tired.

Daniel promised Celey they would stop at the farm after church to see her mother. Celey entered Clarissa's room, and tears welled in her eyes; she looked so frail! Celey carefully sat on the edge of the bed, afraid to jostle her. Clarissa took Celey's hand and tried to reassure her that she would be fine. She said it was just a bit harder carrying a child at her age than when she was young.

Clarissa turned the conversation from her condition to Elenore and Henry. She wanted to knit them a blanket but wasn't sure she had the strength to do it. Celey promised they would do it together.

Celey told her mother all the news from town. She told her what Daniel had said about Mr. Beck acting as if he were having the baby, which made Clarissa laugh. Celey told Clarissa that Nancy and Samuel Kennedy would welcome their new baby any time. Nancy had begun her time of confinement, and Samuel's ma was staying with them.

A soft knock on the door interrupted the women as they shared the news of their friends and neighbors. When Celey opened the door, Jane was waiting on the other side, trying to say 'Gama' and pointing to Clarissa. There was no better medicine to be found than the little girl snuggling next to her grandmother. Again, Celey wished she could draw and capture this moment forever.

In June, Jane turned one. The family gathered at Clarissa and Harrison's to celebrate. Clarissa felt well enough to sit in her rocker while Jane squealed in delight at the rocking horse Daniel had built for her. Celey had painted it bright colors while Henry teased her that he'd never seen a horse with flowers on his coat. The adults were exhausted at the end of the day, from helping Jane and her cousin Jazz 'ride the saucy'.

Alice and Caleb had shared the news that Jazz would be a big brother before the year's end. Everyone was excited about having three new babies by Christmas. In her mind, Celey corrected that number to four. She planned to wait until she was positive before she told Daniel.

When Jazz turned one at the end of Summer, Jane was running. The child never slowed down. At his celebration, he constantly tried to catch his cousin as she ran from one place to another. Levi had promised he'd look after her and make sure no harm came to her.

Celey was thankful to have the opportunity to sit with her mother on the porch. Although Clarissa appeared stronger, Celey noticed that Harrison was always nearby. She never remembered her father being as attentive as he was today. Celey noticed that when a breeze blew across the porch, Father moved to tuck the quilt more tightly around Clarissa's legs. When the sun started to change places in the sky, he repositioned her chair so she could enjoy the warmth of its light. As evening shadows began to fall, Harrison lifted Clarissa from her chair and carried her to her bed. Celey had a sense of dread she'd never before experienced.

Josiah Harrison Dobbs was born on September 15, 1845. Clarissa didn't even live long enough to hold him.

The shock and the pain of losing her mother were almost more than Celey could bear; when she lost her baby, she prayed to die.

Chapter 22

Daniel was at his wit's end. He didn't know how to help Celey. It tore at his heart to see her hurting. He'd done everything he knew to do. He took Jane to his Ma because Celey couldn't seem to care for herself, much less the child. Each morning he did his chores and made their breakfast. He could only get her to eat a bite before he had to leave to work in the fields or help Henry with the logs they were cutting. As he went about his work, he would think of her and worry.

Elenore and Alice had tried going to see her each day, hoping she would talk or cry. They had stopped coming because the reminder that they were both carrying a child while she no longer did seemed to drive her deeper into the pit of grief.

She hadn't seen her baby brother. She'd been too ill to attend her Mother's funeral. Harrison had all he could do caring for a newborn. Amanda was helping in every way she could, but the family was worried they'd lose Josiah too. They had to find a way to feed him. Mrs. McCollister had loaned them a pap boat she'd brought from their store in Ozark, but Josiah was not thriving.

When Daniel sat Celey down and told her that Harrison had married a widow with an infant child just weeks after Clarissa had died, the dam finally broke. She sounded like a wounded animal as the sobs wracked her body. Henry had come running when he heard the sounds, afraid something had happened to his brother.

When she had cried her pain out, Daniel held her. He smoothed her wild hair, dried her face, and prayed for her. *God, I'm beggin' You, please comfort*

Celey's heart. Please take away this fierce pain she's feeling from losing her ma and our little one. God help me to be strong enough to bear what she can't; let me be her strength when she has none. Lord, thank you for giving me the privilege of calling her my wife and blessin' us with Jane. God, that little girl brings your sunshine into every corner of our world, and I ask you to help us to be the ma and pa she needs. God, we ask you to bless Harrison. We know he's missing Clarissa something awful, and we thank you for bringing the Widow Lane to our community when they both needed someone to care for them and be a helpmate. We ask you to strengthen little Josiah and help him grow strong.

They sat quietly for a long time. Celey was letting the words her husband had spoken sink into her heart. When she finally stirred in his arms, she said, *I need to see Father.*

Daniel pulled the wagon into Harrison Dobbs' yard. The man sat on the porch in Clarissa's rocker holding his infant son. Daniel glanced at Celey, trying to decipher how she was doing. He saw a weary smile cross her face as she watched her Father cradle the tiny body in his arms.

Daniel helped her from the wagon seat, and she nearly flew into her Father's waiting arms. Her tears flowed again, but this time they weren't aching sobs. Father and daughter comforted each other as they grieved the loss of the woman who had been their family's backbone. Daniel watched as Harrison introduced her to Josiah; Celey marveled over how much he looked like her mother.

When Josiah began to cry, a woman stepped from the house, a baby in the crook of her arm. *I didn't mean to intrude, but I could hear him starting to fuss.* Celey reached out and took her free hand, *Thank you. Thank you for saving my brother.* The woman smiled and squeezed Celey's  hand. Before they left, Celey walked with her father to the white oak tree beyond the barn to say goodbye to her Mother.

She hugged Harrison tightly before Daniel helped her into the wagon, and they drove away. They were quiet for a time, then Celey placed her hand in Daniel's and said, *Please stop at your folks; it's time to bring our Jane home.* Daniel knew she'd be alright then. There were days when he'd find her crying as she did her chores, but he no longer worried he might lose her too.

Elenore and Alice delivered healthy boys, Rezin Tilman and Ammon Reed; when the family gathered for Christmas, they had much for which to be thankful. As each person expressed gratitude, Celey closed her eyes and remembered her mother sitting by the fireplace last year, holding Jane. The memory comforted her as she reflected on the year and their losses. When she opened her eyes, she looked around at her family. Three years ago, they had been six; tonight, they were twenty. Five families entwined into one. They'd lost some they loved, but they'd gained as well. When her turn came, Celey said, *I'm grateful for you all. Each of you is a strand in the tapestry of our lives.*

Chapter 23

The next few years flowed gently past. Jane grew like a weed and insisted on following her Pa's every step. Despite her Ma's efforts to tempt her with dolls and pretty dresses, most days found her with a dirt-streaked face from tagging along behind Pa and Uncle Henry as they plowed and worked in the fields. Daniel put his foot down when it was time for them to cut timber. Although they were experts at felling the tall pines, there was always the chance that one would turn as it fell. Daniel refused to let Jane be anywhere near when they were getting in logs to the slough.

When Daniel worked in the forest, Celey often took Jane to see her grandparents. Alsey and Jefferson thought the little girl was the most delightful imp ever. She was the only granddaughter, and they doted on her. Other times they took a picnic lunch to Harrison's. Celey and Jane would sit under the white oak, and Celey would tell the little girl stories about her grandmother. After they ate their dinner, they would go up to the house. Jane was fascinated with Josiah and Serena's little boy, Peter, who was only a few weeks older than Josiah. The two little boys were inseparable. Jane being three, thought it was her job to decide what they should play. More often than not, the little boys would end up wrestling in the dirt. If Celey wasn't watchful, Jane would be right in the middle of their fun.

The Fall of 1847 was an exciting time for their little town. Although Jane was still too young for schooling, The Common School Law had been established, and Celey hoped they'd have a public school by the time Jane was ready.

As the years passed, they would reflect on the changes to their lives, family, and community. Four short years ago, Daniel Tilman had rescued a young girl in the mercantile from a scoundrel. Their town had been without a church, and it had been unsafe for women and children to walk down the streets alone. Today they had a lovely little church with a full-time preacher. A doctor had even opened up a practice in the back of the mercantile.

There had been losses; a small graveyard now stood next to the church. New faces were added to their community and congregation, and with the preacher readily available, there had been a flurry of young folks eager to marry. All-in-all, their little community had seen many changes for the better.

Occasionally, someone would catch a glimpse of Mrs. Anderson or one of her older children. It was easy to forget about the Anderson family now that Tom wasn't there to terrorize the townsfolk. On the rare occasions she thought of them, Celey would whisper a prayer for Mrs. Anderson and her children.

The Dobbs family's most exciting events were Levi and Amanda's engagements to Melinda and Robert Powel. The Powel family had moved to Waldron from Lawrence County. Their father, Newton, was a 'Hardshall' Baptist Elder who was making his way to Texas when he settled his family in Scott County.

Lacking a Primitive Baptist church in the area, Arilla Powel and her children attended the Methodist church on Sundays. She felt the Lord was more concerned about them *not forsaking the assembling*" than he was about what they called themselves. Levi first saw Melinda Powel in the Mercantile; she had pale blue eyes and chestnut-colored hair and smiled as if something amused her. Levi was taken with Melinda from the moment he saw her. The next time he saw her, his heart dropped; she was sitting next to a tall young man at church. As quickly as hope took flight, it dashed to the ground.

Levi was sulking near the wagon, confident his life was over and that he'd be a bachelor for the remainder of his days. Amanda's voice interrupted his musings; *Levi, this is Melinda Powel and her brother, Robert. They've recently moved here from Lawrence County.* The beautiful girl with pale blue eyes had a brother!

The four young people quickly became inseparable. Despite his misgivings that they weren't Baptist, Elder Newton Powel held Levi in high regard, and he quickly came to love Amanda as if she was his own.

When Christmas came that year, the family had grown once more. They gathered to worship in their little church, surrounded by friends and neighbors. As was her habit, Celey thought of Mary as the Reverend read from the Word about the birth of Jesus. She wondered at the emotions Mary had experienced during her son's life. Celey knew she would give her own life for Jane's and tried to imagine the sorrow Mary must have felt knowing Jesus must die to save a sinful world.

As the congregation sang *Silent Night*, Celey prayed for God to protect Jane and keep her from harm. She also prayed that God would give her the strength to trust Him no matter what He asked her to face.

Chapter 24

February 1848

Celey and Amanda stood outside the church, waiting for the family's arrival. Amanda's pacing was making Celey nervous. *Amanda, be still; Robert will be here in plenty of time.* Amanda paused, but only for a moment. When the Powel's wagon pulled into the churchyard, Celey was exhausted from watching her sister.

Robert stepped toward his bride, but Celey was faster and shooed him into the church. She turned to her sister and, for a moment, saw the little girl she'd shared a room with and remembered her saying, "Jeesh! *I think I'll pass if that's what love does to you.*" How proud their Mother would be of the young woman Amanda had become. Celey hugged her little sister and said,

Come, Darling, your most incredible adventure is waiting inside.

The ceremony was a simple one. Elder Powel read the vows, and Reverend Logan led the congregation in prayer, asking God's blessing on their union. The weather had been unseasonably warm, and the women served dinner to celebrate the young couple.

As winter turned to Spring, Celey reflected on her life. In a few days, she would be twenty-one years old. At times it seemed only yesterday that she had been the sixteen-year-old girl that Daniel had rescued. Now she was a wife and mother. She and Daniel would be married five years in December, and they had a good life.

Their crops had done well, and their stock had multiplied. Celey's hens laid so many eggs that she sold the extra ones to Mrs. McCollister at the mercantile. Daniel had added a room to the cabin for Jane. Jane was a happy little girl and smart as a whip. She was a delight to everyone who knew her. Not only did Celey have her younger sister Amanda, but God had also blessed her with Elenore and Alice. Soon she would have another sister when Levi married Melinda.

Her father was doing well. Serena had been good for him and the whole family. She had never tried to take Mother's place; she was just there, loving everyone and giving them all time to adjust.

Celey hadn't realized at the time that Serena was hurting too. They had lived in Waldron only briefly when her husband got killed in a logging accident. Serena was left alone in a strange town with a newborn. God brought her and Harrison together at a time of great sorrow, and a deep love had grown between them.

Celey thought about the baby she and Daniel had lost when Mother died. She grieved the child, but the pain wasn't as sharp as it had once been. They had buried him next to her mother under the white oak on Father's farm; it was a comfort to Celey to think that her Mother watched over him. She wondered if she and Daniel would ever have more children. God knew the desires of her heart, but Celey had placed this in His hands, and she would be content, whatever His will.

In May, the family gathered at Harrison and Serena's for the wedding of Levi and Melinda. Melinda loved the farm and wanted a small ceremony with their family. After her father read their vows, the family shared a meal in the shade of the pines.

Quickly the conversation turned to Texas. Newton Powel had decided the time was right to finish his journey. He told them of the reports he had received from neighbors who had already made the trip. *Brother Stuart wrote that the land in Williamson County is so fertile the crops grow three times as large as they do here. He said that the game is so plentiful he has only to step outside to kill a turkey or deer. Brother Harrison, Brother Jefferson, I must see this good land that the Lord has blessed. We will leave for Texas in June; you and your families should also come.*

As the conversation continued, Celey felt a moment of panic. Would Father leave his home in Arkansas? If he did, would she ever see him again? She thought of her younger siblings. Jackson was thirteen, and Josiah and Peter were only three. If Father moved, Jane would be heartbroken to lose her playmates. Celey realized that Amanda and Levi might go as well. Robert and Melinda would want to be near their family just as she wished to be with hers. What would life be like without them here?

As quickly as the panic had risen within her, a sense of peace swept through her heart. Regardless of who stayed in Waldron or moved to Texas, they would always be family. While they might not see each other again on earth, they had the promise of being reunited in Heaven.

Celey looked around at her loved ones. She was truly blessed. Even if Father left, she would not be alone; Daniel and Jane, Ma and Pa Tilman, Henry and Elenore, and Alice and Caleb were her kin too.

In June, the Powels and a small group of neighbors headed to Little Rock to follow the Natchitoches Trace down to Texas. Once they reached Texas, they would follow the Cherokee Trace to Nacogdoches, and from there, they would make their way west to the hills of Williamson County and their new home.

Each time a letter came from Newton or one of the neighbors who had gone with him, there would be a flurry of discussion and planning to join them, but after a few days, everyone settled back into their routine. When Melinda and Levi shared the news that they would be parents in March of 1849, all thoughts of Texas vanished.

As was their tradition, the family attended the Christmas service and assembled at Jefferson and Alsey's afterward. As they enjoyed their feast, they looked back on the year. Word had come from Crawford County that Harrison's brother Ezekiel had pulled up stakes and moved to California.

News of Samuel Brannan's cries of "Gold! Gold! Gold from the American River!" had been a siren call to many in their community. Celey remembered

Levi and Daniel talking about the wonder of simply picking the nuggets up from the ground. She had been concerned - for a time - that their future lay in California, but the men eventually lost interest, as they had with Texas.

As they shared what they were grateful for, they discovered that Amanda and Robert would also become parents in the new year.

Chapter 25

Daniel would occasionally bring home a newspaper from his trips to town. Henry and Elenore would join them for supper; afterward, the adults would sit at the table while Daniel or Henry read the news and the children. Rezin and Jane played in her room.

They found it shocking that land prices in Texas had risen to $10.00 per acre. No one had ever heard of such high prices. More disturbing was the news that the State of Georgia was trying to legalize Polygamy. They'd heard rumors of such a thing out West but not closer to home. They were having a spirited discussion about the country's events when Daniel's face suddenly turned pale.

Daniel's voice shook with anger as he read:

"Proclamation by the Governor,

State of Arkansas

To all to whom these presents shall come – *Greeting*:

Whereas it has been made known to me that TOM ANDERSON, who was indicted at the 1843 Summer term of the Eastern District Court of the State of Arkansas, for the attempted murder of United States Deputy Marshall Jeremiah Hanes and for multiple counts of arson and attempted arson in the County of Scott, and is now wanted for the murder of a guard at the Arkansas State Penitentiary, had escaped from the State Penitentiary at Little Rock and is now running at large.

Now, therefore, I, Monroe S. Hawley, Governor of said State, by virtue of the authority in me vested by law, do hereby offer a reward of FIVE HUNDRED AND FIFTY DOLLARS to any person who may apprehend the said Tom Anderson, and deliver him to the Sheriff of said county of Scott, in order that justice in this behalf may be had and executed.

In testimony whereof, I hereunto set my hand and caused the seal of said State to be Affixed, at Little Rock, on the 19th day of February, A. D. 1849. MONROE S. HAWLEY"

The article continued by describing Tom Anderson; Daniel didn't bother to read it; they remembered his face well.

Elenore had moved to Waldron after Anderson had gone to prison. They listened as Henry quickly told her about Tom and his associates and the mayhem they had caused before Marshall Hensley had arrested them. Daniel didn't realize how tightly he gripped Celey's hand until she winced. In Daniel's mind, her pain was one more thing he had to blame on Anderson.

Henry had taken the newspaper and ridden to his Pa's and the Dobbs' farm. He wanted to warn the men that Anderson was on the loose. Tom had made violent threats toward them all, and they needed to be on the lookout for him. He rode into town and strode into the Sheriff's Office; Bird Jeter wasn't there. On further investigation, Henry found him at the telegraph office, the telegraph operator trying to explain why he'd failed to deliver the message he'd received three days earlier about Anderson's escape. Henry wanted to hit the man but knew it would do nothing to change the situation.

After warning the rest of the family, Henry headed home. He found that Elenore and Rezin were still at Daniel and Celey's; Daniel had refused to let her go to the cabin until Henry returned.

Daniel and Henry discussed how best to keep their families safe until the recapture of Anderson. The women could no longer go to town or visit family without one of them accompanying them. The brothers had been cutting timber but agreed they should stay closer to home. When you lived on a farm, there was always some chore or repair needed so they wouldn't just sit idle.

Celey enjoyed having Daniel around the cabin; Jane was ecstatic. With every step that Daniel took, her little legs followed. He taught her how to milk the cow and let her gather the eggs. He would laugh until tears rolled down his cheeks as she chased her Ma's chickens around the pen until she caught one by the tail feathers. Celey scolded them both that her hens would stop laying if Jane didn't stop tormenting them, but she would laugh at the site it made when they weren't nearby.

Each evening Jane would crawl into her Pa's lap, and he would read to her from her book of rhymes or tell her stories about when he and Uncle Henry were little boys. Jane would always beg for '*just one more*' when Celey told her it was time for bed. They always gave in, and Celey would tell her about Grandmother Clarissa and how she loved Jane very much. As Jane said her prayers, she asked God to bless Grandmother and to let her see her again someday.

Rumors were all there were of Tom Anderson. The Sheriff had been up to his house, but Mrs. Anderson had been tight-lipped about his whereabouts, and he saw no evidence of Tom having been there. No one had seen him, and there had been no incidents to make them suspect that he was in the area. Still, Daniel kept a watchful eye on Celey and Jane. He felt the only thing keeping Anderson at bay was the Governor's reward. Many more folks would be looking for him and willing to turn him in because of that five hundred and fifty dollars.

In May, news came that someone had seen Tom with a group of "Forty-Niners" headed to the gold fields of California along the Missouri Route. They'd all read the reports of the sufferings of those who journeyed by the Northern crossing. Cholera was a scourge along this route, with accounts of mass graves on the prairie a regular event. Vegetation for the livestock was scarce, nothing but scanty grass and stunted cedars for one hundred and fifty miles West of the Missouri river.

Daniel hoped it was true that Anderson had gone West. He knew he'd never feel completely at ease until he saw for himself that the man was either in prison or dead. He asked God to forgive him for wishing for the latter.

With no further news of Tom Anderson being in the area, the family returned to their daily life. Levi and Melinda's baby, Johnathan, was a precious little butterball. Jane would beg to hold him. At five years old, she thought of herself as the 'grown-up cousin' and spent her time being a 'momma' to all the little boys. Jazz would remind her that he was almost as big as her, but he adored his cousin and gladly went along with whatever she said they should do.

Amanda's son, Alexander, was born during the winter's first blizzard. When the family gathered at Christmas, Robert held his son as he recounted the story of Alexander's birth.

Mandy knew her time was close, but she wasn't ready for Ma or the Doctor. When she woke me and it was time, the wind was howling, and the snow was so thick I couldn't see to get to the barn. I was sure scared. I couldn't get to Ma's, and all I could think to do was pray. Mandy kept telling me everything would be fine and that babies were born every day. She told me to build a fire in the stove and get some snow to melt in that big stew pot of hers. I was digging at that snow like a mad dog, tryin' to fill that pot up and make sure I didn't get too far from the cabin. All of a sudden, I heard a cry. I didn't know what had happened, but I dropped that pot where I stood and ran inside. There was my Mandy, holding this little feller. She grinned at me and said, "See, I told you babies were born every day." Amanda added that he hadn't found her stew pot until the snow had melted two weeks later.

Celey held her youngest little nephew and longed for another baby. She was thankful for Jane, the little girl was the world to her, and Celey knew that if she never had another child, Jane would be enough. Still, she missed the feel of a tiny body cradled in her arms. A single tear slid down Celey's cheek when Serena told them she was expecting a child in July.

Chapter 26

The new year brought one of the worst winters they'd had since 1845. Henry again brought his stock into Daniel's barn, and the two families rode out the storm together. To pass the time, they played Charades, a game Elenore had read about in a Jane Austen novel. Jane and Rezin thought it was hilarious to watch Daniel and Henry act like bears and lions while they tried to guess what they were.

When Henry recalled the winter storm of 1845 and how he had been sure he'd miss his wedding, the children were quiet as a mouse. Rezin was more concerned about his papa's horse 'Old Buster' slipping on the ice than he was about Papa makin' it to town in time to marry Mama.

After a few days, the snow stopped, and they let the children play outside for short periods. Daniel and Henry reminded Celey and Elenore of little boys as they threw snowballs and helped the children make snow angels. By mid-January, Henry's family could move back home. There were other storms but none as bad as the first one. Each time snowflakes fell, Jane and Rezin would beg for them to 'live together' so they could play the funny pretending game.

On a warm Sunday in March 1850, the women of their church organized a social after the worship service. Spirits were high as everyone looked forward to the chance to visit with neighbors and catch up on the latest news. Because of the earlier storms, many of their congregation hadn't been to church since Christmas.

Reverend Logan had spoken to them about God telling Abram to get out of his country and to leave his family and his father's house and go to a new land. Celey had never thought much about this story until she heard Levi and Robert tell her father that they would leave for Texas in April.

Newton had written to his children that land in the Milam District, where he lived, could be had for fifty cents an acre. They only had to live on the forty acres for five years; then it was theirs. Newton told them of the fertile soil and how good his crops had been. He encouraged them to make haste as the land around him was selling quickly.

Celey listened in horror as her brother and sister talked with Father about their decision to move. Levi encouraged Harrison to join them. He knew his Father wanted to see Texas. Levi turned to the others in the family and invited them to come along. He joked that if they all went, they'd have enough folks for their own wagon train.

Celey felt relief when Father said that with Serena expecting a child, he didn't feel it would be safe for her to travel. Harrison wouldn't risk losing his wife and child.

When Alice came to visit, Celey was pleasantly surprised. The women didn't see each other often enough, but Alice had two active boys, and they lived several miles away. Celey tried to drop in to see her when they went to town. Mostly she saw Alice on Sunday after church when their large family met for dinner. With all the small children and babies, they rarely had a chance for a nice long talk.

The children had been given a treat and were playing in Jane's room. Alice wandered around the cabin, stopping to run her fingers over the curtains she'd helped Celey sew what seemed an age ago. Celey was beginning to worry when Alice came to sit next to her and took her hand. *My sister, how I love you and how I'll miss you when we move to Texas.* How would Celey ever stand so many of her family moving that far away? Jane would be devastated that Jazz was leaving. The two of them were excited to start school in the fall finally. Celey knew they were a little scared, but they had each other; now Jane would be alone.

The women reminisced for hours about their life in Waldron. They laughed about their surprise double wedding and marveled at how much their community had changed since they were mere girls of sixteen.

Though she was sad that her sister was leaving, Celey became caught up in Alice's excitement about the new adventure. Alice begged Celey to join them. She was sure her brothers would love Texas, and they could all be together. Alice knew if they all went, Pa and Ma would come too. As much as Celey loved Alice and would miss her, she prayed that Daniel would want to stay in their home. She didn't want to leave Father.

With Summer came the news that the family had reached Texas. They had purchased farms and were busy building cabins and getting in crops. Newton had been right; Texas was a good land. Despite his daughter's urging, Jefferson Tilman remained in Waldron. He had kissed her forehead and told her that his wanderlust days were over, but he was proud that she was bravely seeking this new land.

Daniel had never considered leaving; he loved their home and wanted to stay near his parents and Celey's. Henry and Elenore had almost gone with them until they discovered Elenore was with child.

Jane was excited to start school in the Fall. She begged Celey or Daniel to help her with her letters and numbers every day. Jane insisted she must be able to read and write before she started school, even though Celey explained that she was going to school to learn those things. When classes began in September, Jane could write her name, say her alphabet, and count to ten. She fancied that she could read a bit. Celey was sure that Jane had memorized the nursery rhymes she pretended to read.

On her first day of school, Celey braided Jane's hair and tied it with new ribbons from the Mercantile. Daniel had bought her a shiny little pail to carry her lunch. They all rode to school that first morning, and as Jane eagerly skipped toward her class, Celey felt the quickening of the child she carried.

Henry picked Jane up from school; the little girl talked non-stop - *her teacher, Mr. Magruder, had told her what a clever girl she was, and Dorothy Riley was the youngest girl in school but could already do her sums - would*

Uncle Henry help her learn her sums? She was older than Dorothy and should know hers too. When they reached the farm, Henry said, *Jane, I do believe you talked my ear plumb off.* Jane looked at her uncle with a puzzled expression as she checked to be sure he still had both ears.

Jane repeated the events of her day for Celey. When Daniel returned, she scrambled into his lap and shared her day with him. Celey looked at the two people she loved most and smiled as she thought how pleased Jane would be when she discovered she was to be a big sister. Celey had decided to wait a bit longer before sharing her secret with either of them until she was sure.

In October, they had gathered at Harrison and Serena's. The harvest was in, the weather had been mild, and Harrison had gotten a letter from Amanda. All these things were reason enough for a celebration. The group was the smallest it had been in several years; ten of their number were in Texas now. Celey held her baby brother, Gage, as Harrison read Amanda's letter to them.

"2 Sept 1850
Williamson County, Tex
Dear Father and all the connection,
I take pen in hand to let you know that we are all well and doing well. Robert and Levi have had a great adventure. Nearby there are a great many wild horses, Mustangs, the Texians call them. Levi and Robert built a corral and went about driving the horses into it with the plan of gentling them and selling them to the ranchers nearby. Father Powel told them that the horses had been wild far too long to be gentled enough to ride, but Levi thinking he knew best, was bound to try.

After capturing nearly twenty head of the poor things, the men begin trying to ride them. I must confess that I have never felt such terror and knew that they would most surely be killed. Melinda begged Levi to turn them out, but he was of a mind to continue. After three days of trying to put his saddle on one of the wild creatures, he and Robert devised a narrow pen just big enough for one horse. The ruckus they caused trying to get a single horse into that pen was almost more than my heart could endure. At long last, they were able to trap one of the poor things in the pen, and they closed a gate behind it.

The horse whinnied and cried at being confined so, but Robert was able to get his saddle on it. Oh, the jumping and bucking the horse did at that. It went near crazy trying to separate itself from that saddle.

Levi kept talking gently to it, and he and Robert risked life and limb to stroke its mane through the bars of the pen. After what seemed an eternity, the creature seemed to have given up its fight. Robert climbed on its back, thinking he would ride it a bit. As soon as Levi opened the gate to its little pen, that pony exploded in all directions at once.

Robert flew through the air, and Levi narrowly escaped a nasty kick to his ribs. Father Powel advised them to let the creature loose before it made Melinda and myself widows. I was surely glad when they realized the

wisdom of his words and gave up their notion of being cowboys.

Father, you must write to me as soon as you get my letter and tell me of the kin. I expect that if all has gone well, I have a new brother or sister, and you must tell me all there is to know. Kiss Celey for me and give my love to all.

I remain affectionately your daughter

Amanda Powel

To Harrison Dobbs
Waldron Arkansas"

Knowing they had not been hurt, everyone laughed about Levi and Robert's attempt to be cowboys. Harrison shook his finger at Jackson and warned him not to think of trying such nonsense, even if he could find a wild horse.

Serena took out a quire of paper and began a letter to Amanda and the Texas family; since they were all gathered, they could each send their regards. Jane wanted to tell Jazz about her school and the friends she was making, but she missed him and wished he was there to sit next to her. Grandma Serena wrote her words for her, and then Jane signed her name. Daniel, Henry, and Elenore sent their 'Best Regards' to all the kin; Henry said that Levi and Robert must write to them about the crops and the market prices. Serena asked Celey if she had anything to add. *Yes, please tell Amanda that she's going to be an aunt again next year.*

Daniel pulled Celey, still holding Gage, into his arms and spun her around the room. Jane wasn't sure why Pa was acting that way, but Gage was laughing, and it looked like fun; she hoped he would twirl her around too. Jane got her wish when Daniel swung her up into his arms and said *Jane, you're going to be a big sister!*

At the Christmas service that year, Jane again thought of Mary. How frightened the young girl must have been giving birth all alone, yet the Bible made it sound as if she was serene. Celey thought about the birth of this baby. Who would be there for her? Mother had been with her when Jane was born. She knew Elenore and Serena would do all they could to comfort and help her, plus they had a new doctor in town.

As long as Daniel was nearby, everything would be fine, no matter who else might be there.

Just in time for Celey's birthday in April, a parcel arrived from Texas. Celey had never received a package by mail. They celebrated opening it, taking care not to rip the paper and twine and smoothing it all to reuse one day. Inside were the most beautiful items. Amanda had sent a quilt for the new baby. Celey had planned to use

Jane's little quilt; now, the baby would have its own. Melinda and Alice had knitted socks and a little cap. Jazz had even drawn a picture of the wild Mustangs as a present for Jane.

Daniel had brought Jane's cradle in from the barn. He and Jane had spent hours polishing the wood. Celey wasn't sure who was more excited about the new baby, Jane or Daniel. Jane was hoping for a sister; at nearly seven years old, she was still the only girl. She loved all the boys but thought it would be wonderful to have a baby sister *"like Ma had Aunt Mandy."*

In the evenings, they would discuss what they would name the baby. Jane wanted to call her sister Victoria because Mr. Magruder, her teacher, had told them about a princess named Victoria. Daniel would tease her that the baby was sure to be a boy, and he would call him Jehosephat or Rumplestiltskin. Jane would squeal and say, *Pa, if I have a brother, you mustn't call him either of those names; he would never learn to spell them.* Daniel would agree, then quickly come up with another tricky name to spell. Celey loved watching the two of them. Jane was the light of her Daddy's life, and the little girl thought her Pa was the strongest, most handsome, smartest man in all the world.

Celey knew that Jane was excited about the new baby, but she was concerned about the little girl having to share her Pa. Jane had been an only child for nearly seven years. Many times, she had spent her days following Daniel's every step. Celey prayed that Jane wouldn't feel that Daniel wasn't giving her the attention he always had when there was a new little one in their home.

Daniel and Jane continued their game as Celey stitched a nightgown for the baby. She thought how glad she was that Daniel was teasing about the names for a boy. At least, she hoped he was teasing.

Chapter 27

Tom Anderson had spent the last two years hiding from the law; his luck had been bad since he'd run off from prison. Tom had begun plotting his escape when they'd put him with a group of convicts leased out to work the road.

They'd been working near the river; Tom had thought that if he could get free of the guard, he could slip aboard a steamboat and make his way back to Scott County. Daniel Tilman and Harrison Dobbs were why he'd gone to prison, and there was a score to settle with them.

Tom had made out like he was sick; Boss Tackett had sent him to the treeline so as not to foul the area where they'd been working. Not much had gone the way he had planned. When the guard came to check on him, the men had struggled. Tom had Boss Tackett down, choking him, and somehow Tackett had gotten his gun from his belt, but before he could shoot, Tom had clouted him on the head with a rock.

There hadn't been time to stick around to see if the guard was alive or dead. Tom had escaped his chains, taken Tackett's shirt and gun, and beat a path through the woods. He had known they'd set the dogs on him and hang him if he didn't make the river.

He had stayed near the tree line when he got close enough to hear the water. He'd seen a barge loaded with crates and barrels about fifty yards away. After slipping into the water, he'd held onto one of the guide ropes until they were close enough to the far side of the river for him to swim to shore. Tom had hidden in the river weeds until the barge was out of sight, then made for the timber, planning to put distance between himself and the prison.

The sun had been setting when he slowed down. He'd ditched his prison shirt several miles back. Tackett's gun was useless unless he found some dry bullets, but he'd figured he could use it to scare someone if he had to. His most pressing need had been food. As hungry as he'd been, even the slop at the prison had sounded good. He'd found some berries and picked the bush clean, but he'd needed more to eat.

As the moon rose, he'd come across a small cabin. He remembered smelling wood smoke and side meat cooking. His empty belly had made sounds like a hungry bear. He'd made his way closer; news of his escape probably hadn't made it this far into the sticks, but he couldn't be too cautious. He was almost to the porch when Tom felt the barrel of a shotgun press into his back.

The voice that had said, *"Who are ya? What are ya doin' sneakin' round here?"* had belonged to Grady Ellis. Tom's luck had just gotten a whole lot better or as bad as it could get.

"It's Anderson, Sheriff." Tom had waited for the shotgun blast but hadn't been prepared for Ellis to grab his shoulder and spin him around. Ellis had stared at him a long time before he spoke again; seven years in prison hadn't been kind to Tom. His hair had greyed, and his face was gaunt. *"Let's git inside."*

Ellis put a plate with side meat and corndodgers in front of Tom, who had been trying to keep from gulping the steaming cup of coffee he held. It had looked like he lived alone and hadn't done much more than throw a blanket on the cot and some wood near the fireplace. There had been a few tins on a shelf near the stove. Tom had noticed it was missing a leg; someone had shoved a large rock under the corner to hold it up.

Tom had taken the first bite and felt his stomach knot up. He hadn't had any meat in a long time, so he'd made himself go slowly; it would have been a shame if he'd gotten sick. Ellis had stared at him while he ate, and Tom had begun to make a plan just in case he needed to run for it.

"How'd you get out of prison? Who's after ya?" Ellis had asked. Tom had told the story of his escape, keeping his eyes on Ellis for any sign of trouble. When Tom had finished the story, Ellis had said, *"You can bed down on the floor tonight, but you best get movin' at first light."* Tom had decided to take his chances; he took the old quilt Ellis had scrounged up and stretched out near the fireplace. Neither man had slept

that night, each keeping an ear out for the other.

At dawn, Tom had left, taking some corn fritters, sidemeat, and three bullets from Ellis' gun when he wasn't looking. Tom had kept moving in a Northwesterly direction. He wasn't sure how far he'd come but knew getting on the water; he'd make better time.

A keelboat had pulled up to the bank; the sail on the cabin had come loose and twisted. Tom had watched as the Captain worked to free it and decided to take a chance. *"You there, you be needin' some help?"* Tom and the Captain had straightened the sail and secured it. *"Could ya be using some company? I'd be willin' to work for my meals."* Tom asked. The Captain had nodded, and they'd cast off; he had felt a bit better, reckoning he'd be safer on the water than tryin' to go it on foot.

It had suited Tom fine that the Captain wasn't a talker; he'd wanted to get as far from Little Rock as possible and figured the less he talked to folks, the better. He would have liked to know about Boss Tackett, though.

They'd traveled for two days without seeing anyone. Occasionally there'd be folks standin' on the bank wavin' as they passed, but Tom had made sure to be on the far side of the boat whenever that happened. Late evening on the second day, the Captain had told Tom they'd be pulling into Clarksville in the morning. When he'd heard the Captain snoring, he'd eased into the water and made for shore.

Tom had made his way to Clarksville; he needed food and wanted to know who was looking for him. He'd stayed to the back streets; before he'd gone far, he'd seen a handbill nailed to a post. Tom couldn't read much but recognized his name and that somebody had a big reward out for him. He'd cursed as he tore it down; how was he supposed to get supplies with those blame things nailed up everywhere?

When he heard a bell ringing, he figured out it was Sunday. He just needed to find some do-gooder's house, and he could get what he needed. At a cabin on the edge of town, he'd filled a seed sack with food and supplies. He'd taken bread, jerky, dried fruit, tobacco, coffee, and a pair of pants; in the barn, he'd found a horse. He'd figured he couldn't do much worse than murder, so he took the horse and rode North to Missouri. He still had kin there, and they'd help him lay low till he could figure out what to do.

Seven years of plotting to go back to Scott County would have to wait for a mite longer; the Marshall would be sure to look for him there.

He'd had a few close calls. Those notices had made it up to Berryville by the time he'd gotten there. His brother, Lem, at Shell Knob, hid him out a few days, but his Missus had raised a ruckus, and Tom had moved on.

That's how he'd ended up out in California. He'd needed to get far away until things simmered down. He'd overheard some fellas talkin' about *'pickin' gold nuggets up right off the ground.'* Tom had managed to get in with the fellas and had made the long trip West. Along the way, he'd thought he'd die. Cholera had spread through the wagon train, and they'd buried a fair number of folks along the trail. He'd been pretty sick but had somehow managed to beat it.

When they'd made the gold fields, Tom had realized that if there ever had

been gold layin' about, it was long gone. Still, he and his fellas did right good; Tom had put together a pretty good-sized poke in the two years he'd spent in California. Of course, if his associates had ever figured out that he was stealin' bits of their gold, they'd of shot him.

Tom had left the goldfields and made his way back East. When he'd gotten close to Waldron, he'd cut through the timber to his still site. No one had been up there in a long time. His barrels were dry, and the hoops were loose; nothing a good soakin' wouldn't fix. His still would take a site more work to set right; his coil was busted, and the cap was missin'. After a bit, he'd found it out in the woods; probably some critter had wallered it around.

Tom had known it would be risky to go back to Waldron, but the way he looked at it, Tilman and Dobbs had beat him out of eight years. He'd broken his back bustin' rock in prison or the gold fields when he coulda been sittin' at his whiskey still, makin' money and sleepin' in a warm bed at night. He owed Yates too; he'd turned on Tom tryin' to save his worthless hide. Tom didn't know where he'd got to, but if he came across him, he'd settle their score.

He'd watched his house for a couple of days; he didn't want to take any chances on the law bein' around. He'd seen his Missus and a girl hangin' out the wash. He reckoned she was his youngest, Emily; she must be pert near sixteen.   The rest of his young'uns would be growed and gone by now.

Tom had waited till it was dark before he'd gone in. His Missus was none too happy to set eyes on him. She'd got religion while he'd been gone. When she'd tried to make him leave his own house, he'd given her a shove that had shut her up. Tom had torn the cabin apart looking for his whiskey, but the fool woman had busted all his jugs; she wouldn't be bustin' up anything else. He told the girl to fix him some food and tell him about the goings on in town.

He'd had to give her a shake or two to remind her that if she didn't want what he'd given her ma, she best not hide anything from him. The girl told Tom the men were getting logs into the slough close to Tilman's farm and some nonsense about buildin' a school.

She told him Harrison Dobbs' wife had died, and he had a new wife and some young ones. Then she told him what made the last eight years worth livin', that oldest Dobbs girl, had married Daniel Tilman. The girl told him Tilman had a little girl and his wife was carrying another child.

Chapter 28

The late snow and Spring rains had turned the road from Daniel and Henry's farms to the church into a mud pit. Deep ruts from heavy wagons carrying logs to the mill for the new school had made the road nearly impassable. The ground had dried enough that the men had set aside a day to fill and smooth the ruts. They would plow the damaged road and smooth out the dirt, filling in the tracks, then drag heavy logs across it to pack it down.

Since they hadn't been able to take the logs by wagon, they'd been getting them into the slough; then they'd float them on the Poteau River to the mill. The whole community was excited about building a school. They'd been meeting in the church, but with so many children, they needed more room.

As they had done with the church, there was a day planned for building and fellowship. Jane was beside herself with anticipation. She'd heard her ma, pa, and Uncle Henry talk about when they built the church. Jane loved school. Mr. Magruder was strict, but he taught them so many exciting things. Jane was the only small child in her family who attended school. When they all got together at Grandfather and Grandma Serena's house, she would collect the younger children and "teach" them their letters.

Next year when Josiah, Peter, Rezin, and Ammon started school, she didn't want them to be embarrassed, so Jane made them all learn to write their name and count to ten. She was the only girl, so the boys usually let her have her way. They all adored her. She loved them all, but she especially loved and missed her cousin, Jazz, who lived in Texas. Jane often wondered what it would be like to visit Aunt Alice in Texas and see Jazz again. Maybe one day when she was grown, Pa said he'd never leave Arkansas.

Celey was ready for her baby to be born. She was so big she could never get comfortable. Her back hurt all the time, and she was tired. Father teased her that she was carrying twins; after all, he was a twin. Celey didn't know if she was expecting two babies, but she felt enormous and clumsy. Daniel would wrap his arms around her, and his fingertips were farther from touching every day. Each night as she struggled to get comfortable, Celey prayed that God would protect her baby and bless it. She prayed for a safe birth and that she and Daniel would be good parents to the baby and Jane.

On Monday, the men would meet at the Tilman's to get the rest of the logs moved down the river from the slough. Next Saturday, the community would meet to build the school. Jane had begged her ma to let her stay home and watch; she was fascinated by how they used poles to keep the logs moving. When Celey had told the little girl that she needed to learn how to read and write more than she needed to know how to float logs down the river, Jane had stomped away to the wagon to wait for her pa.

When Daniel let her off at the schoolhouse, he told Jane that God wouldn't like her being mad at her ma. Her ma was doing what was best for her, and it made her sad when Jane behaved poorly. Jane promised Daniel she'd apologize that afternoon. She hugged him tightly and skipped away to her friends. Daniel had looked in on Celey when he brought the wagon home. She'd fallen asleep in her chair, her knitting in her lap. He placed a quilt over her and kissed her lightly on her forehead, trying not to disturb her.

When Daniel reached the slough, Henry had just started pushing the felled trees into the current. Jackson Dobbs, Samuel Riley, and Simon Reed were on the far bank, ready to guide the logs from there. Jefferson and Harrison were on the bank, watching the men work, but their sons insisted they stay away from the heavy trees. Things were going well until mid-morning. One of the trees had gotten sideways and caused a jam. They'd tried to push it loose, but it wedged. Daniel would have to walk out onto the logs to free it. He hated this part of moving logs by water. There was always a chance the log would roll when it broke free of the jam; if he wasn't quick on his feet, it could crush him.

Jackson and Henry offered to clear the jam, but Daniel was already making his way over the makeshift raft formed by the logs. Using his pole, he pushed against the tree blocking the others. He felt it move and pushed harder. Daniel

braced himself for the roll, preparing to jump if necessary. Instead of rolling, the log dipped in the water when it was free. Daniel quickly regained his balance, turned to wave to Henry that they were clear, and fell face down on the logs as a gunshot came from the shore.

Henry got to Daniel first, though hampered by the movement of the giant floating trees. Simon had kicked his horse into a gallop when Henry yelled, *Get the Doc!* Henry realized his pa was trying to make his way onto the logs. *No, Pa, it's too dangerous.* Jackson had reached them and realized they had to stop the logs from moving, or they'd never get Daniel clear. He and Samuel started pushing against them, trying to cause a jam. By the time they could slow them down and get one turned, they were covered in sweat, their arms and legs shaking.

Jackson and Henry lifted Daniel and began the longest journey of their lives. They feared the massive floating trees would suck them under with each step. One misstep, and they could all die. Harrison had his hand on Jefferson's arm as both a restraint and a reassurance. They didn't need to try to go out there. Henry and Jackson were having a hard enough time matching their steps. Harrison had a bad feeling as he silently prayed. Daniel hadn't moved or made a sound since he'd fallen.

They buried Daniel the next day. At the graveyard, Jane clung tightly to her mother's hand, her tiny body shuddering. Celey wondered how she would ever console the child. Daniel's death had broken her heart. Alsey Tilman had never seen her husband cry; his sobs had echoed across the graveyard. She'd clutched Henry's arm when he started toward Tom Anderson, where he stood in the trees. She'd lost one son; she couldn't lose another.

Chapter 29

Father had insisted that Celey and Jane move into his house. With Anderson back in the county, Harrison wanted them close by. Doctor Purtle had told him that Celey was in shock. She moved about like she was in a trance. If Jane needed something, Celey saw to it. If someone spoke to her, she answered. She sat in her mother's rocking chair the rest of the time and stared into the distance.

Jane had been inconsolable. Henry had held her for hours while the little girl had cried for her pa. They were so worried about the child they'd sent for the Doctor again. He had assured them that with time, Jane would be fine; Harrison wasn't so sure. When she'd fallen asleep, Henry carried her to Serena's bed; her grandma didn't want her to wake up alone. Harrison sat up all night and watched Celey stare at the fire. Just past midnight, he noticed the silent tears sliding down her cheeks, and his heart ached for his girl. He rose to start a pot of coffee, and as he passed her chair, he paused and laid his hand on her shoulder. *God will provide.* He whispered.

The days ahead had no beginning and no end. They had voted to dismiss the school. With Tom Anderson nearby, no one felt safe. Those who had lived there eight years ago remembered when the women and children couldn't go to the mercantile without their menfolk.

Bird Jeter had sent for the U. S. Marshall; everyone was relieved when Marshall Hensley and Deputy Hanes arrived. They went up to Anderson's place and were shocked by what they found. Anderson's daughter, Emily, was bound to a chair, a large yellow bruise across her cheek. A few feet away lay the body of Mrs. Anderson, cold and lifeless.

Emily told them about Tom coming home. When her ma had tried to make him leave, he'd knocked her down. Her mother had struck her head against the hearth, but Tom wouldn't let Emily see to her. He'd made her tell him about everything that had happened since he'd gone to prison and was especially interested in the Dobbs and Tilman families. He'd tied her up when he left so she couldn't warn Daniel Tilman of his plans.

Bird took Emily into Waldron so Doctor Purtle could look at her face. He and some other men would return to the cabin for Mrs. Anderson's body. They'd bury her in the graveyard next to the church. Emily had begged them not to bury her at the cabin. Marshal Hensley and Deputy Hanes were going to search the area for Tom. Hensley didn't expect to find him but wanted to look at Anderson's old still site.

There were fresh tracks around the still site that led north. Hensley and Hanes followed them but lost them at Sugar Creek. He knew Grady Ellis was over near Crystal Mountain; the Marshall from Little Rock had already paid him a visit. Ellis had denied seeing Tom, but the Marshall and local Sheriff were going to keep an eye on him. Hensley had heard that when Chambers got out of prison, he'd headed West. The Marshall wondered where Gus Yates was these days; no one seemed to know what had happened to him.

Two weeks after Daniel's murder, Celey gave birth to twins. Jane named her baby sister Victoria Abigail. Celey named the boy Joseph Daniel. Jane had said that it was almost like Jehosephat. Celey and her children were still living with Harrison and Serena. Her father refused to allow her to return home until Anderson was caught or killed.

Although the community tried to return to normal, no one could forget that a murderer was on the loose. Marshall Hensley had returned to Fort Smith; Deputy Hanes was staying on for a while. Even though there was an uneasiness about it, life had to go on. Work on the school continued - when they finished the building, the townfolk came together for a celebration.

Celey remembered the earlier days. She thought about the time she'd spilled coffee on Daniel's hand and the dozens of times since they'd worked and fellowshipped with their friends and neighbors. She felt weary as she thought about how much had changed in eight years. She was worried about Jane; her little girl was so withdrawn. Nothing they did seemed to help her. Celey had thought the birth of twins might ease her pain, but Jane withdrew even further. She had given her one of Henry's barn kittens as a special pet, hoping that caring for it would draw her out. Jane fed and watered it  but never sought it out to play, despite the kitten following her every step.

Celey didn't know Jane had come up until the little girl threw her arms around her and started to cry. *Jane, whatever is wrong?* Celey asked. *Oh, Ma, I'm sorry; I didn't mean to make you sad. I forgot, I promised Pa I'd tell you I was ashamed for being mad at you the day he...* Jane sobbed against her ma, unable to continue.

Celey held her daughter, stroking her hair until she calmed her. *Baby, you don't ever make your ma sad. I am so sorry that you have been carrying this burden.* Celey hugged Jane and reflected on the blessings in her life. A Godly man had loved her, and they had three healthy children. She had family and neighbors who cared for her. She didn't know her future, but she was certain God would provide.

Chapter 30

Summer in Scott County was hot and dry. Elenore and Henry visited often and brought vegetables from the garden she and Celey had planted. The watering trough Daniel and Henry had built for them was the only reason there was such a good harvest. Even though Jackson and Harrison helped Celey in the garden at the Dobbs' farm, she had declared they would only harvest weeds; the vegetables were withering in the sun.

Henry suggested they build a trough from the pump to the garden. They wouldn't be able to water the entire garden, but they could save some of it. While Henry and Jackson found some lumber, Celey and Harrison started raking the dirt into hills to form a pathway for the water. They decided to try to save the collards, beans, and squash, everything else they could get from Elenore and Celey's garden. Jane, Rezin, Peter, and Josiah played under the white oak tree near Clarissa's grave, a favorite spot of Jane's. Elenore had gotten the twins and Gage down to sleep and was helping Serena prepare the noon meal. For the first time in weeks, Celey felt that she could breathe. Since losing Daniel, she'd felt like her lungs wouldn't hold the air she needed.

Working alongside her father, Celey was enjoying his company and listening to Jackson and Henry laugh when water from the pump splashed in their faces. No one had noticed the man who'd ridden into the yard.

Dobbs, I warned you that you'd be sorry for not selling to me. Before Henry could reach the rifle, he'd leaned against the well; Tom Anderson had shot Jackson and ridden away.

Everyone but Henry ran to where Jackson lay. Henry grabbed his rifle, mounted his horse, and galloped away in the direction Anderson had fled. As Jackson took his final breath, Harrison held his son and vowed that Tom Anderson would pay whatever the cost. His head jerked up when he heard the shot in the distance.

Jefferson Tilman had heard the shots that came from the direction of the Dobbs' farm. He had harnessed the horses to his wagon and climbed up on the seat when Henry's horse, Old Buster, came galloping into the yard. Jefferson saw Alsey drop to her knees at the sight of blood on the saddle. Henry couldn't be dead; they'd lost one son, and he couldn't live through losing another. He slapped the reigns across the horse's backs and raced toward Harrison's. About a mile down the road lay Henry.

The parched ground drank in the blood from the bullet wound in his shoulder, something he would recover from in time. His left leg lay at an unnatural angle from the rest of his body, broken in the fall from Buster. Henry begged his pa to go to the Dobbs' farm and check on Jackson, but Jefferson refused to leave his son. With great effort, the two of them managed to get Henry into the wagon bed; Alsey arrived on Buster as they pulled away.

Not knowing her son's fate, Alsey led his horse to the barn where she'd climbed on the hay bales to reach his back. She had never ridden a horse, but Buster seemed to know how important this was and had stood perfectly still as she struggled into his saddle.

Jefferson had used Buster's saddle as a cradle for Henry's broken leg. Alsey was sitting in the wagon's bed, holding his head and trying to keep him from jostling around too much. She fervently prayed they'd make it to Doctor Purtle's without Henry being in too much pain. They hadn't gone far when he'd passed out; Alsey thanked God for granting him this relief.

At the Dobbs' farm, everyone was inside. Elenore had collected the children, and Jane was reading to them in her grandma's bedroom. Celey, Serena, and Harrison had moved Jackson's body into the barn and covered him with a quilt. Harrison was debating between staying with his womenfolk and going to look for Henry when Elenore ran from the house. Jefferson had pulled his wagon into the yard, Henry's horse tied to the sideboard. She scrambled into the back, careful not to jostle her husband.

Harrison rode into Waldron for the doctor; they feared the jarring wagon ride would be too much for Henry. They had pulled the wagon into the barn to conceal it; Jefferson stood at the door with Henry's rifle while Elenore and Alsey saw to Henry; he still hadn't woken up. Celey stood staring toward the pump where earlier her younger brother and Henry had laughed and joked. A monster moved among them, a thief, stealing the most precious thing of all, lives.

Harrison arrived at his home with Doctor Purtle, Bird Jeter, Deputy Hanes, Samuel Riley, and Elenore's father. John Beck had never seen his daughter in such a state. A smear of blood stained her cheek. He knew it wasn't hers; still, it frightened him to see it. Henry was a good man, a devoted father to Rezin; God just had to let him be alright. His family needed him. John noticed the quilt off to the side, and his heart broke for the Dobbs family. Jackson was a fine young lad who was always laughing and smiling. The world would be a darker place without him in it.

Henry came around when Doctor Purtle started examining his shoulder and leg. The doc was afraid to jostle him around and went to work on him in the wagon. He gave Henry some laudanum and started to remove the bullet. Before he set Henry's leg, the doctor gave him another dose. After Doctor Purtle finished his operation, he examined Jackson's body. The bullet had hit him directly in the heart; the doctor said he was dead before he hit the ground.

The Sheriff, Deputy Hanes, and Samuel Riley had gone back to where Henry had fallen from his horse. They found tracks going through the woods for a few yards, but they disappeared before long. Somehow they had to find Anderson before anyone else was hurt or killed. The men rode back to Harrison's as Anderson watched from the trees. All those years of hiding in the forest with his still had made Tom a ghost.

They moved Henry into the house, and between the laudanum and the pain, he'd passed out again. Celey and Serena had prepared Jackson's body while the men built a coffin and dug a grave near his mother. Harrison had insisted the women stay inside with the children. They had lowered his son's body into the grave while the Doctor stood by with a rifle, just in case. After the hasty burial, Deputy Hanes headed back to town. Bird and Samuel were going to the Tilman farm to check on the stock. There was an uneasiness that they couldn't shake.

Celey found some clean clothes for Elenore and sat with Henry while she changed and looked in on her child. Rezin was asleep in Serena's room with the other children. Serena called out to her from the kitchen, insisting that she eat; Elenore hadn't realized she was hungry until she took the first bite. Henry was sleeping when she walked back into the boy's room, where they'd settled him. Celey would check on her throughout the night, and Elenore was always sitting by Henry's side, her lips moving in silent prayer for her husband.

Doc Purtle had spent the night. He wanted to keep an eye on his patient, and it was safer not to be on the road. Jefferson and Harrison had set up with him in the kitchen, drinking coffee and talking. Alsey was sharing Celey's room. Her mother-in-law had cried herself to sleep while Celey whispered words of comfort to her as she would a child.

The next day, Celey wrote to their family in Texas. She hadn't realized how hard it would be to tell them about Daniel and Jackson's deaths.

"July 10th A. D 1851

Dear Brothers & Sisters

I Gladly embrace the present opportunity of writing you a few lines To let you know that we are all well through God's mercy - hoping these Few lines may find you all enjoying the Same blessing of providence.

We received your letter of the 17th of June, which gave us great satisfaction to hear that you were all well at that time and well Satisfied and doing well. I hope you may still remain to enjoy that *peaceful Satisfaction of mind which is the greatest Blessin' in this life.*

I am living with Father on petty game and doing the best I can for My Self. If you have not heard, I will Now let you know that I lost my husband on the 6th day of last May. He was Shot While he was at work about one Mile from our cabin getting logs down the river to the mill. His Brother Henry, Pa Tilman, Father, Jackson, Samuel Riley, and Caleb's brother, Simon, were with him. Daniel was out on The logs when he was Shot. Daniel turned to wave to Henry and After he was Shot fell on his face and never Spoke. He lay there till Henry and Jackson could get him off the logs. Simon rode for the Doctor, but it was too late. Father Saw the glimpse of some person Run off and said he could tell for certain who it was That had done the murder. It is a great loss to me, the greatest I could have met with in this world.

Tho, I am not left without friends entirely yet. Father will do a good part By me, I am living at this time in the house with Him. His family is all well except Josiah. He has the chills & fever at this time, But it is not very bad, and he is able to go About a good part of his time & is now Taking Medisan to brake it.

After Daniel Was killed, I got Carson Murdoch to Administer on the estate, and it was valued at $6.30, and I took my Dower out and there was $3.30 left to pay the Debts. The property that I selected was two yoke of oxen at sixty Dollars, two Horses at 80 Dollars, 4 cows and calves & one heifer at 35 Dollars, & one hundred & twenty-seven Dollars in money, Which was my portion of the estate. So you can see that I am not left entirely destitute of something to live on within myself

I should be glad To see you all once more and live By you, but being left in the Situation that I am in, I never expect to See you in this life unless Father should move to that Country. I would Be very willing to come if he would Move to that country. Tho he talks of little else but moving at this time, I think if he could sell to his notion, he would move to Texas. There is too much sorrow in this place.

I will now inform you that Tom Anderson is not Satisfied with taking Daniel's life. He is still seeking more Blood. Father and I were working in his garden on the 9th day of July. Henry and Jackson were building a trough to water a portion of it because the draught has been so fierce.

Tom Anderson rode into the yard with a gun on his Shoulder and said to Father that he would be sorry for not selling to him. Before Henry could reach his rifle, Anderson shot Jackson without any ceremony, and he died a Few minutes after Anderson Rode off

To Pa Tilman's. Henry rode after him, and We heard a shot while Father, Serena, and myself got Jackson's body into the barn. Not knowing what Anderson might try next, Elenore had gathered the children into the cabin. In a short time, Pa and Ma Tilman rode into the yard with Henry in the wagon. Anderson had shot Henry in the shoulder. The impact knocked Henry from his horse, and he suffered a badly broken leg. Father rode for the doctor. The doctor says Henry's leg will heal, as will the bullet wound.

The men built a coffin for Jackson and buried his body near Mother. Father would not let us women go out to the grave for fear Anderson might return. Anderson is now the great monster of the West

I suppose you have heard that I have two more children. They were Born on the 19th of May 1851, a son & Daughter. Daniel had teased Jane that he would name a boy Jehosephat, so I called him Joseph Daniel, And Jane named the girl Victoria Abigail. They are fine healthy children And are growing off very fast. They Will Soon be sitting alone if they keep Their health. Jane is in good health.

Tom Anderson's youngest Daughter died on the 26th Day of June. She had been Sick for several Days and was thought to be Nearly well. She was Struck with the Dead Palsy and only lived about 36 or 40 hours. There has been a good deal of sickness in this County this summer but very few deaths from it.

Celey Tilman To

Levi Dobbs & Melinda
Caleb Reed & Alice
Robert Powel & Amanda"

Chapter 31

Tom had been up to his cabin; the girl had been gone, and so had his Missus. He hadn't bothered to look around for a grave. He'd got wind that the girl had died too. It didn't matter to him if she had; now, there was no one to raise a ruckus about his whiskey. He wanted a smoke but couldn't take a chance on lighting his pipe and the smell giving him away; he'd run out of whiskey some time ago. Tom had never been a patient man, and it had cost him more than once.

Tom had been watching Dobbs' house for several days; no one had come out much since they'd buried the son. He'd thought his aim was better when he'd shot Tilman; now, he'd have to find a way to finish him off. It would have been good to have another man to help, but all his clan was either dead or had turned on him. Chambers was out West somewhere, and no one would ever find Gus Yates' body; Tom had made sure of that. Ellis was a different matter. Tom would have to go carefully there. Ellis had been thick with him and the rest until he'd gone to prison. Tom knew if Grady Ellis got him in his sights again, one of them would end up six feet under.

Anderson had ridden over to Tilman's farm; he'd planned to set fire to it, but that Deputy Marshall was always hangin' around along with some men he'd pinned badges on. Tom was curious why none of them 'lawmen' were here at the Dobbs' farm. He'd watched close; there was no one there but the women and children, the two old men, and Henry Tilman, and he was busted up. He hadn't seen the doctor in a couple of days. Maybe Tilman was already dead.

Celey was too restless to sleep. She slipped on Daniel's coat; it made her feel close to him to wear it and eased through the door onto the porch. The night was too warm for a coat, but she felt safer - like Daniel was watching over her. So much had happened in the past few days. Celey wondered if she'd ever truly feel safe again. She remembered all those years ago when she'd first met Daniel. She had been scared of Anderson back then, but knowing that Daniel was there had given her comfort; he had been like her guardian angel. Celey had felt threatened since Tom Anderson had murdered him. Daniel and Jackson were dead, and Henry was gravely wounded, all because of one man and the sin of greed.

She knew Father wanted them to stay in the house, but she just needed a few minutes to clear her mind. She'd sit in Mother's rocker and think about her

Father's words. Father and Pa Tilman were making plans. Father had talked of going to Texas before; this was different. Jackson's death had made him determined to go. Pa Tilman had said he'd never leave Arkansas; now, he regretted that he'd ever come to this place.

They would wait for Henry to heal; they couldn't travel with his leg like it was. While Celey would love to see her brothers and sisters and live near them again, it was hard to think of those they would leave behind. Who would care for the graves of her loved ones when they were no longer here? She'd be leaving behind her life with Daniel, the cabin he'd built for them and her garden, so many things. Celey knew those were only things and that what mattered were the memories she carried with her no matter where they lived. Still, it would be hard to leave them.

Celey wanted Jane and the twins to be safe. She realized that no matter where they lived, there would be dangers but what they faced here was too much. Father was right; the best plan was for the family to move to Texas. It would be easier if they were all going. Father was going to write to Uncle Ezekiel's son, Jake, over in Crawford County to ask if he was interested in buying their farms. It would be a comfort to know that their kin owned this place. Celey knew she would see Daniel, Mother, Jackson, and the babies again in Heaven, but knowing that family might be here to tend them made leaving easier. She'd meant to sit in Mother's rocker and think, but without realizing she was doing it, she'd begun to pace. Tom noticed a movement on the porch and edged closer.

It was Tilman's widow.

After Anderson had murdered Jackson and shot Henry, Deputy Hanes had sent John Beck to Ozark to send a telegram to Marshall Hensley in Fort Smith. The Marshall had met his Deputy at the Tilman farm, and it was there that he caught sight of Anderson. Hensley followed Tom, almost losing him twice. Anderson had gone back to the Dobbs' farm but left after a few hours. The Marshall followed him to his cabin; from there, Anderson headed north toward Booneville. He'd gone a few miles through heavy timber, making it almost impossible for the Marshall to follow. When Anderson stopped, he went to work, digging. He'd dug a good-sized hole when he suddenly stopped and looked around. Hensley had worried that Anderson had somehow spotted him. After a few minutes, Tom had moved some brush aside, and the Marshall saw him drag a body lying on a blanket to the hole he'd dug. Hensley was pretty sure it was

Gus Yates but would have to come back to be certain. He marked the spot in his mind and watched as Anderson dumped the body into the hole and covered it with dirt and brush. Hensley wondered if Tom would go after Ellis next and wished there was a way to warn the Marshall from Little Rock.

Tom headed back south, this time taking an easier route. When they reached Sugar Creek, Hensley had to hang back so Tom wouldn't hear him cross the water. He hoped he'd be able to pick up the trail on the other side. Tom had ridden through the water downstream for a way before he came out on the other side. The Marshall had found his tracks and headed after him. This time he did go back to Harrison Dobbs' farm.

Anderson had settled into the treeline, and Hensley had found a place further away where he could see Tom and the house. He knew from his

Deputy that the family was only coming outside when necessary, so it was quiet for a good while. The Marshall watched Tom drink his whiskey and chew on his pipe stem, but he never lit the pipe. He could tell Tom was getting antsy. His impatience had been his undoing before; Hensley hoped that would be true again.

Marshall Hensley had been surprised when Daniel Tilman's widow had come outside. At first, she'd sat in a rocking chair close to the house. He hadn't worried too much about her since he had a clear line of sight on Anderson. When she'd started pacing, he felt the little prickle he got at the base of his neck right before a fight.

When Celey started moving, so did Anderson. He'd never finished his business with her, and her husband wasn't around to interfere this time. Tom made his way closer to the house, staying to the treeline when possible, often stopping to be sure there was no one else around. If he could make the end of the porch, he could hide in the shadows until she passed by him, and then – like before, things hadn't gone according to his plan…

Harrison Dobbs burst through the door, not knowing what he'd find. There had been a shot, and they'd heard Celey's scream followed by the heavy thud of a body falling on the porch. He found her standing over the lifeless body of Tom Anderson, Jefferson Tilman at her side. Marshall Hensley was running toward them from the treeline.

Chapter 32

Jefferson had caught sight of Anderson earlier in the evening. He'd said nothing because he didn't want to alarm the family. When he realized that Celey had gone outside, he panicked. Jefferson had slipped out a window with Henry's rifle and eased his way around the house; he'd broken into a run when he realized that Anderson wasn't where he'd been hiding earlier. Just as Anderson stepped up on the porch, Jefferson caught sight of him and prayed his aim would be true as he took the shot. Celey's scream had terrified him.

Marshall Hensley told them he'd been following Anderson for several days. He'd wanted to tell them he was out in the timber watching the house but couldn't without tipping Anderson off.

Hensley had watched Celey come outside; when Anderson started toward her, the Marshall had gotten into position to shoot. He'd been about to squeeze the trigger when he'd seen the muzzle flash and heard the shot that killed Anderson.

Jefferson Tilman's words from eight years ago had turned prophetic – *"If anything happens to my boys or any of mine, you'll know the wrath of God firsthand."* Jefferson hadn't known at the time that it would be his hand that God would use to render justice for the murders of his son, Daniel, and Jackson Dobbs.

A few weeks later, The Tilman and Dobbs families loaded their wagons to move to Texas. Even though the danger was gone, Harrison and Jefferson agreed it was time to move on. They'd made many wonderful friends here; their family had become one and grown here. They had loved and lost; now it was time to join the ones waiting for them in Texas.

Ezekiel's son, Jake, had agreed to buy the farms. Now that Anderson was dead, Jake was considering buying Crenshaw's old place and some others that had belonged to Tom. None of the Anderson children that had moved away wanted anything to do with Waldron or Scott County.

As the day of their departure grew closer, Celey visited the graveyard next to the church and Daniel's grave; she'd already been to the white oak tree to say goodbye to her mother and Jackson. She stood at his grave and reflected on her life since Daniel Tilman rescued her eight years ago. Much had changed in the town where they lived. They had built a church and a school; there had been marriages, babies born, and deaths. Many times she hadn't understood why things had happened the way they did, but she'd always trusted in her Heavenly Father to care for her and her family. God had blessed her with a godly husband and three healthy children. Most of all, she had hope that one day, she'd see her loved ones again.

On the morning of their departure, they were a group of sixteen with five wagons - Harrison, Serena, Josiah, Peter, and Gage Dobbs; Jefferson and Alsey Tilman; Henry, Elenore, and Rezin Tilman, John Beck, Elenore's father; and Celey with Jane, Joseph, and Victoria. Simon Reed was driving Celey's wagon. He had decided he wanted to try being a Texas cowboy.

Harrison stood at Clarissa's grave, remembering their journey from Illinois to Arkansas almost twenty years ago. Some of their neighbors had come by to wish them well and express their sorrow at seeing them go. Celey knew that she would never see these people again. She hugged Nancy Riley, and they promised to think of one another on their shared anniversary. Celey tucked a small package into her wagon from Mrs. Reed for her Texas grandchildren, Jazz, and Ammon, as Mrs. Reed was cautioning Simon to stay away from those wild Texas horses and be a farmer like his father.

When they'd given the last hug and wiped away the last tear, Reverend Logan called for their attention and said a prayer over their journey. *Dear God in Heaven, we ask that You look down upon our brothers and sisters as they journey from this land into the unknown and make their way to family in Texas. God, we ask that You protect and keep them along the way. We thank You, Father, for the blessing of family and friends, and while we are sad to see these friends leave us today, we are thankful for the hope that we will one day be together again.*

Harrison walked toward them from where he'd stood under the shade of the white oak. When he reached Celey's wagon, he stopped to help her climb aboard. Before he released her, he looked into her eyes and said, *God, will provide.*

The trip to Texas was uneventful. Until they reached Nacogdoches and headed west, they could have still been in Scott County, except there were no mountains. As they got closer to Williamson County, Celey's excitement grew. She was going to see Amanda and Levi again and Alice! She had missed Alice so much, especially after Daniel was murdered. It had been Alice who announced that Daniel was going to ask permission to call on her. The women had shared a surprise double wedding; they'd shared secrets and fears. It would be so good to have her near again.

Levi had found a farm for Father near his own at Gabriel Mills. The farmer had gotten gold fever and was anxious to sell. There was a comfortable house for Father and Serena and their growing family. Serena was expecting their second child in the Spring. Levi told them there was a smaller house on the farm, about one hundred yards from the main house. It would be perfect for Celey and her children for now.

Jefferson and Alsey were going to live with Alice and Caleb. After everything that had happened, Alice insisted on her parents being in her home.

Henry and Elenore were going to stay with Levi and Melinda until they could build a home on their farm. Once the house was built, Elenore's father, John, would live with them. In the meantime, John would stay with Celey's sister, Amanda, and her husband, Robert.

By far, the most excited was Simon. Caleb had arranged for his younger brother to live and work on a nearby cattle ranch. Caleb was going to be a real cowboy!

The reunion had been noisy; everyone was talking at once. Even Arilla and Newton Powel were joining in the festivities. Newton offered a prayer of thanks for the safe arrival of the family. The food and fellowship went on for hours as they talked about all that had happened the past year. Reluctantly they cleared the tables and made preparations to go to their separate homes. Since Harrison's family had homes ready to move into, Caleb, Robert, Levi, and Simon went to unload their belongings; the other wagons could wait.

Work began on Henry and Elenore's house immediately. With the family eager to help, they should be settled before the first cold spell. Celey was enjoying having her family all around her again. It seemed like a lifetime since they had been together, and so much had changed.

Jane was nervous about her first day in a new school; she wondered if her new teacher would be like Mr. Magruder or if the children would make fun of her. Celey had reminded her that Josiah, Rezin, and Peter would also be new students and that her cousins, Jazz, and Ammon, would be there. Celey prayed that being in school with the other children would bring Jane out of her shell.

Long before Christmas, everyone was settled into their new homes. Excitement mounted as they planned this first Christmas together. They would all go to church, and the entire family would meet afterward at Harrison and Serena's for dinner and fellowship.

As Newton Powel delivered the message on Christmas morning, Celey thought of Mary as she often did this time of year. How had Mary been so strong? She had willingly accepted that she would give birth to the Christ child and that he would one day die for the world's sins. Celey thought of her twins and was confident she would never have the strength or the faith to sacrifice them for another willingly. She breathed a silent prayer of thanks to God for His wisdom in choosing Mary.

Back at Harrison's, the gathering was boisterous. The young children were excited because they knew there would be small presents for each of them after dinner. Levi wondered how the babies could sleep  through the noise. No one minded how loud it was because it reminded them how blessed they were to be together under one roof.

After eating, they talked about what they were thankful for and all the changes in their lives. Celey longed for Daniel as she listened to Elenore express her gratitude for Henry being alive. This first Christmas without Daniel had been difficult. She'd put together small gifts for Jane and the twins, but her heart had not been in it. She was appreciative of their home at Father's, and she did have the means to support her children for a while, but she found herself worrying about what she would do when she had exhausted her funds. Celey knew her Father and family would never let her do without, but she couldn't expect them to support her when they had their own families. She was certain she would never remarry; losing Daniel had broken her heart. She would have to think of a way to provide for her children. Father walked up behind her as if reading her mind and whispered, *God, will provide.*

Chapter 33

George Marcus had a houseful of rowdy boys. There were times he'd go to the barn so he could hear himself think. As she cared for the baby, another boy, his wife, Sarah, would laugh at him and say, *"You'll miss their antics when they've grown and moved away."* It was a wonder to George that the child could sleep, but he did. They'd never had such an easy child as Abner.

The family had come to Texas from Missouri in 1852 when Abner was one. George had heard about what a vast and fertile land it was, and he also liked the idea of milder winters for his family and his stock. They had settled near Gabriel Mills in Williamson County because there was a water-powered gristmill. George thought this would help him make a bigger profit on his harvest if he was close enough to haul his wheat and corn to be ground instead of paying someone else to do it.

Although his boys were young, James, the oldest was only twelve; they loved to help their Pa. George had often redone their 'help,' but that never stopped him from letting them work beside him.

Moving to Texas had been an adventure. Most of the families that had started the trip from Neosho had left them in Fort Smith, Arkansas; many joined wagon trains to the gold fields of California. George had thought that would be a grand thing to see, but he had a family and wasn't a young man at thirty-nine. By the time they reached Nacogdoches, only one other family was traveling with them, and they had decided to settle there.

George and Sarah had considered finding a homestead there, but they felt drawn to continue their journey West. When they reached Williamson County, they knew they were home. George had set about building them a cabin, and with the boys helping, it had only taken a bit longer than he'd planned.

The community welcomed them, and the boys started school. Each day they came home with stories about their new friends from Arkansas. Even though Jazz and Ammon Reed were younger than him, James was impressed that their uncle, Simon, was a real-life cowboy. George had found the boys behind the barn one day acting out a story that young Jazz had told them about his father and uncle trying to ride a wild Mustang. George didn't know if it was true, but his boys had a time trying to put a makeshift saddle on their dog. Today James had told his father, *"Jazz says that everything in Texas will bite ya, stick ya, or sting ya!"*

George had met the Tilman and Dobbs families at church; they were kin to Elder Powel somehow. He hadn't had time to get to know anyone except Harrison Dobbs. He still had a great deal of work around his farm and had no family nearby to help. Sarah had told him part of their family had been murdered in Arkansas, and that's why they came to Texas.

One day, as he and Harrison Dobbs had been waiting to unload their grain at the mill, the men had talked about their lives before coming to Texas. Harrison had told George about Tom Anderson and how he'd murdered his son, Jackson, and his daughter, Celey's husband, Daniel Tilman. George admired Harrison's attitude about his losses; he didn't think he could be as forgiving.

The church at Liberty Hill had never gotten into the habit of having community dinners or socials, and the congregation wasn't as close as the one that the Tilman and Dobbs families had left behind. Harrison had noticed this right off with George Marcus. The man needed help but didn't feel close enough to his neighbors to ask. Harrison had brought this up at their next meal together as a family. Immediately Alice and Amanda agreed that a monthly dinner was just what they all needed. The community would be much better off if they were all neighbors and friends. Arilla Powel nodded her approval, silencing her husband's protest that *'the Lord's Day was not a time for parties.'*

The following month, there was a time of fellowship after the morning service. Folks who had sat side by side listening to the Word of God now sat next to one another, sharing a meal.

Even Newton had to admit that the time had brought the congregation closer together. Hopefully, the next time someone in their community needed help, they'd be more comfortable asking.

Harrison had told his sons about George Marcus needing to finish the roof on his barn, and the men agreed they would meet at his home on Saturday to help. Harrison and Serena rode over to talk to George and his wife, Sarah. Harrison was going to offer their help with the roof, and Serena wanted to assure Mrs. Marcus that no one expected her to feed all those men.

At first, George was hesitant to accept their help. He'd always made do on his own. Even in Missouri, they hadn't had close neighbors or family, so he always found a way to do what he needed alone. When Harrison asked George what he would do if one of their community needed help, George finally agreed it would be nice to have them there. Serena explained to Sarah that she and the girls would provide the food if she could make sure there was coffee. They all had small children, but Sarah had five energetic boys, and Serena noticed that Sarah seemed a bit unwell.

Saturday morning, the men headed to Marcus' farm at first light; the women would be along in time to serve the noon meal. George was surprised at how quickly the work went when he had seven other men helping. They had almost finished when the wagons with the women, children, and food arrived.

In no time, Henry and Levi had cobbled together a temporary table and benches for the adults; the children sat on quilts under the trees. Laughter and conversation filled the air as the Marcus, Tillman, and Dobbs families broke bread and talked about what they had accomplished that morning. The conversation turned quickly to why each family had moved to Texas.

Sarah's parents had died a few years ago; she and George had no other family in Neosho. They didn't have close neighbors, and the winters had become increasingly hard on Sarah. The cold, damp air made it difficult for her to breathe; each year, it seemed to take longer for her to recover once Spring had come. Her doctor had told them she needed to live someplace warmer and drier. They had considered going to California, but with five young boys and Sarah's health, the arduous journey had seemed too much.

Henry had told their story. Sarah gasped as he spoke about the sorrows their family had faced at the hands of Tom Anderson. They were glad to be in Texas with the rest of their family and happy to have such good neighbors as the Marcus family.

The adults were enjoying an afternoon of getting to know each other when the older children asked to go to the river; they were in sight of the adults, and George told them the boys played there all the time. The older boys ran screaming and laughing to the water's edge; Jane followed at a slower pace.

James showed their new friends how to skip rocks. You had to find the perfect stone; it had to be smooth and flat, then you flicked it across the top of the water, and it skipped. When no one was successful, the boys decided to 'fish' for polywogs. Trying to 'skip' the rocks was the first thing Jane had shown interest in since Daniel died. She wasn't ready to stop and was determined to learn how to make them skim across the water.

Thomas Marcus had found a stick that suited him and was tying a piece of string he'd had in his pocket to the end.

Soon the boys were squealing as they took turns trying to catch polywogs and minnows on the hook that James had contributed. Ammon was impatient for his turn and started trying to catch anything that wiggled or swam with his hands.

Jane had grown tired of the boys and all the noisy splashing and found a place where she could watch without getting wet. While sitting there, she noticed a woman in the distance. Jane had never seen anyone like her. She wore her black hair in thick braids. Jane thought it odd that the woman's dress

only came to her ankles, and some kind of boot covered her legs. The front of her dress had the prettiest design Jane had ever seen.

As Jane was staring at the woman, trying to figure out who she was and why she dressed like that, the woman's head snapped up. Jane looked in the direction the woman was looking and saw her aunt and uncle running toward the river. James was yelling; the strange woman was running toward him - a knife in her hand.

The woman got to the children first, and Jane watched in terror as she grabbed Ammon's arm and cut him with her knife. The woman reached into a pouch she wore around her neck and took something out, which she placed on Ammon's arm where she'd cut it. Uncle Levi and Uncle Caleb reached the children, and they were yelling at the woman. Mr. Marcus got to them, and Jane heard him saying, *No, no, it's alright; she's trying to help.*

When Aunt Alice and the others made it to where they were, Mr. Marcus had calmed everyone down. He was explaining that the woman was a Comanche named, Manita. She was their friend.

While Ammon was playing in the water, a snake bit his arm. When Manita heard James yelling for his father, she ran to help the little boy. Manita had cut Ammon's arm where the snake had bitten him, and then she placed a Mad Stone on the bite. Mr. Marcus explained that Mad Stones would draw out the venom. Mrs. Marcus had held Aunt Alice back when she'd tried to push the woman away from her son.

Manita put another stone from the pouch on the wound when the first one fell off Ammon's arm. After the second one fell off, Manita put something strange looking on Ammon's arm and tied a strip she'd cut from her dress around it. Mrs. Marcus let Aunt Alice go after that. Alice immediately pulled her son into her arms and started rocking him. Manita placed her hand on Alice's arm and shook her head. She said something in a strange tongue and then acted out being still. Aunt Alice nodded.

Uncle Robert had ridden into Gabriel Mills for the doctor. When they returned, Alice was sitting in the back of the wagon with Ammon in her lap. She was doing as Manita said, being very still. The doctor examined Ammon's arm and declared that there was nothing else to do for him. He told them that what Manita had done probably saved the boy's life. Alice looked around for Manita, wanting to thank her, but the woman was gone.

Chapter 34

Helping the Marcus family with their barn, the church socials, and Manita saving Ammon's life solidified the bond between the families. Sarah Marcus looked forward to Alice and the others ladies stopping by to visit. Living in a house full of 'men,' Sarah was often lonely. These new relationships brought her a joy she'd never known. Her heart broke for Celey and her daughter, Jane. Sarah could see that the young woman was adrift without her husband. She had a large loving family, but it was plain that she grieved for her Daniel. The little girl was terribly withdrawn. She played with the other children, but Sarah had never seen her genuinely smile or laugh. Sarah prayed for Celey and Jane each time they crossed her mind.

One day, Serena asked Celey if she would take some fresh bread she'd baked to Sarah. Sarah wasn't feeling well, and Serena was nearing her time of confinement. Celey hitched up the wagon and set off to deliver the bread. She thought about Sarah and her house full of boys; Celey didn't know how the woman did it. She had all she could handle with Jane and the twins, Victoria and Joseph; she couldn't imagine having five boys. They were good boys, but they were so rowdy. She didn't remember her brothers being that way.

Her thoughts turned to Daniel as she guided the horses toward the Marcus farm. She wondered what he would have thought of Texas; it was so different from their home.

Sarah had been telling Celey about Manita; she lived a little down the river from them and had been gathering plants that her tribe used as medicine the day the snake bit Ammon. Manita's husband was killed in a raid a few years earlier, and she was still mourning. She had learned a few words of English, but mostly they managed to understand each other by acting out what they wanted to say. Sarah told Celey about a time when James had cut his leg. It wouldn't heal, and the doctor had been worried that he might lose it. Manita had come to the house after seeing the doctor; when she saw James' leg, she had mixed up a poultice. In two days, his leg had begun to heal.

The women visited most of the afternoon. Celey noticed that Sarah seemed tired and had a lingering cough. She asked Sarah if they could pray that she would feel well soon.

In late Spring of 1853, Serena gave birth to Elizabeth Ann. Celey had hoped the baby would pull Jane out of her grief for Daniel. Jane would come home from school the first week and walk to Grandma Serena's. She would hold the new baby, her aunt, and visit with her grandma; Celey had a glimmer of hope that her little girl would be alright. When Jane stopped going, Celey was at her wit's end as to how to help her child. Daniel had died almost a year ago; Celey struggled daily with the pain she felt at that loss. In her frustration about Jane, Celey became angry at God.

When she was alone, she would rail in her mind about how unfair it was that Daniel had been taken from them. She questioned God as to why men like Tom Anderson were allowed to harm others. Celey began to withdraw from her family. When they would gather for meals or celebrations, she would find an excuse not to go. The more her anger took hold, the more distant she became, not realizing that Jane was retreating further into her shell because of Celey's actions.

Harrison didn't know how to help his daughter. No matter what any of them did, Celey and Jane slipped further away. Harrison questioned his decision to move to Texas; maybe if they had stayed in Arkansas… Not knowing what to do, Harrison prayed. *God, please help my girls. Please heal their broken hearts. Your Word says in Psalms that You will heal the brokenhearted and bind up their wounds. God, my girls need their wounds bound up. Please, God, we don't know who or what will help Celey and Jane, but I trust that You do.*

Elizabeth was three weeks old when James Marcus rode into Harrison's yard. His ma had sent a little cap she'd knitted for the new baby. Sarah had told James to extend her best wishes and to apologize that she hadn't been to see them. James told them his ma had been feeling poorly and had been in bed for about a week. He assured them they were fine. He and Thomas were helping their pa with the chores and tending to his ma. Serena wrapped up some bread and side meat and sent it with James. She told him to tell Sarah that the girls would be over with some food the next day, then sent Josiah and Peter to Melinda's to let her know that Sarah needed help.

James was untying his horse when he saw Jane sitting under a tree, a black and orange cat was rubbing against her side, but Jane was ignoring it. The cat started rubbing against his legs when James walked up to them; when he leaned down to scratch its ears, it started purring. *Nice cat, don't think I ever saw one colored like this. Whatcha call it?* Jane told him the cat's name was Callie because it was a calico. *Whatcha doin' out here?* Jane told him she was sitting and thinking about her home in Arkansas and her pa. *That makes you sad. Ma always tells us that the things that make us saddest are the things we love the most.* James climbed up in the saddle; as he rode away, he turned and smiled at Jane. *James was nice;* she thought, *when he wasn't with his brothers.* Maybe they were so loud and rowdy because there were so many of them.

Celey had been to visit Sarah and was sitting on Father's porch telling them about their conversation. Sarah had confided that she was afraid she was going to die. Sarah had said she wasn't scared of death; she knew she'd be in heaven when that happened - Sarah was afraid for George and her boys. Celey recounted her words for them, *"Whatever will George do? He's such a good pa, but how will he ever manage five boys? The older boys are in school, but Abner isn't quite two; how will he work the farm with a baby?"* Celey had tried to comfort Sarah, but the injustice of Sarah's situation worsened her anger over her own loss.

Sarah is a good, Godly woman; why is God punishing her and her family? It makes no sense that George and her boys will have to suffer! Harrison's heart broke for Celey. He had lost Clarissa when Josiah was born. He missed her, and he still loved her, but God had provided by sending Serena into his life. Serena had lost her husband and struggled to raise Peter in a strange new place. Harrison believed God had brought her there because He knew they would need each other. Harrison said a silent prayer for Celey and George Marcus. He hoped God would provide for each of them as He had for him and Serena.

A few days later, Sarah Marcus died in her sleep.

Chapter 35

George Marcus didn't know how he would ever survive the loss of his wife. He had been twenty-seven when they married, and Sarah was seventeen. Something about the young woman struck him, she was full of life, and he had always been somber. Maybe it had been the way she teased him about being a grump because George rarely laughed. God knew what He was doing when He brought them together. George was the level-headed one; Sarah found fun in everything they did.

Raising a houseful of boys had been quite an experience. Sarah encouraged them to run and play every chance they had. George remembered being much quieter as a child. When he said anything about how rambunctious the boys were, Sarah would laugh at him and say, *"You'll miss their antics when they've grown and moved away."* She often told him she wanted her boys *"To enjoy their life, not just live it."* They were good boys, always willing to help and they rarely complained or fought with each other. If he were truthful, George enjoyed their boisterous ways.

The first wagon pulled into the yard as the neighbors started to arrive for Sarah's funeral. George looked around for his sons and saw them standing beside the tree where they would bury their mother. James held Abner, and Lil' George held a bunch of flowers they'd picked for their ma in his small hand. George had asked Jefferson Tillman to speak over Sarah. Elder Powel often said things about the uncertainty of death that George disagreed with. George was confident that his Sarah was in Heaven.

George gathered his boys around him, taking Abner from James. The 'men' stood together as Jefferson spoke. *The Good Book tells us in John Chapter 14, Verses 1-3*

"Let not your heart be troubled: ye believe in God, believe also in me.

In my Father's house are many mansions: if it were not so, I would have told you. I go to prepare a place for you.

And if I go and prepare a place for you, I will come again, and receive you unto myself; that where I am, there ye may be also."

As much as we grieve the ones that leave us, we know we'll be together again one day. God, we ask that You comfort our brother, George, and his boys. Help them in the days ahead to remember that You love them and that one day they'll be together again with their dear wife and mother. Amen.

Serena knew that it would be hard for George, with Abner being so small.

She offered to have the little boy stay with them for a few days while George figured out what to do. She told him it might be good for Abner to be around Gage, Joseph, and Victoria for a little while. Reluctantly he agreed. He wanted his family together but had to admit it would be easier to figure everything out if Mrs. Dobbs looked after Abner.

The days that followed were difficult. George had helped Sarah with the boys and the house, especially the past few weeks. Not having her there made everything chaotic. The first morning he burned their breakfast and fed them cold biscuits and cheese. The next day they left their lunch pails and had to go back home for them, so they were late for school even though he'd taken them in the wagon. George wasn't sure how Sarah had kept them so organized. After dropping them at school, he drove to the Dobbs' farm to see Abner before he got to work.

Abner was at Harrison's daughter's little house. Harrison explained that when it came time to go to bed, Abner had cried because he had to leave Jane. The little boy had taken to her and followed her every step. He'd gotten so upset that Celey had suggested letting him stay. Harrison was about to take Gage to her so he could play with the other little ones, so the two men made the walk together. When Harrison asked George how he was doing, George shook his head.

Honestly, I don't know how I will make this work. George told Harrison about the past two days and about how he felt as if he were drowning. Harrison remembered that feeling from when Clarissa had died after giving birth to Josiah. His children had been older, and his daughter, Amanda, had helped with the baby. Still, he was sure grateful when God had sent Serena to him. They were both grieving, and Harrison thought that had helped them heal. He placed his hand on George's shoulder and said, *God, will provide.*

Abner was sitting in the middle of Celey's floor with a cat and a delighted look on his face. The cat was looking for a way to escape. When Abner heard his pa's laugh, he released his 'victim' and ran to George. Gage had wiggled free of his Father and was searching for the escaped kitty. George thanked Celey for looking after Abner and apologized for him being a burden to her. Celey answered. *Children are never a burden, Mr. Marcus. Abner is a wonderful little boy; honestly, I think it was good for my Jane to have him here.*

Joseph ran into the room, and the boys began to play a spirited game of chase. George started to correct Abner, but Harrison shook his head. Celey was laughing, and Harrison didn't want her to stop!

Chapter 36

As the seasons changed, so did Celey's heart. The anger she had held to so tightly began to fade. She still missed Daniel and thought of him often, but now her memories were bittersweet. She spoke of him often to Jane, hoping that talking about her pa would help the little girl.

The Saturday before school started back up, the whole family came over when Serena and Alice had a birthday party for Josiah and Jazz. Harrison had invited George and his boys, and when Serena discovered that Thomas' birthday was between the two other children, it became his party too.

Alice had baked an apple cake for the children, and Celey fixed her mother's recipe for cold biscuit puddin'. Sixteen children ran and played in Harrison's yard as their parents and grandparents watched. Celey watched as Jane played with Abner. Jane was as taken with him as he was with her. She loved Victoria and Joseph, but Abner had stolen her heart. Celey jumped when George said, *Your Jane has been good for Abner. Thank you for letting him stay with you so much these past weeks. I don't know how I would have survived without the help. Come Monday, I've arranged for Manita's daughter to watch him. I know you have your hands full with your own young ones.*

Celey didn't know what to say. It made perfect sense for him to have someone keep the little boy at home. George had to drive Abner over to her house each morning; his older boys would walk to and from school with Jane, Josiah, and Peter; in the evening, he would pick them up. That was wasting time George could be working on his farm. If someone watched Abner at home, the older boys could walk straight to school from their house. Celey realized that she'd come to care for his boys and would miss seeing them every day. Jane would be so sad; she adored Abner. Celey realized that he'd also stolen her heart and choked back a sob as she replied. *Oh, well, that will be so much easier for you. I know it's been difficult. Abner and all the boys will have to come to play whenever they can.* Celey turned away before he could see the tear slide down her cheek.

Without Abner dogging her every step, Jane withdrew into her shell. It broke Celey's heart to see her so sad. The truth was, they all missed him. Joseph and Victoria had cried for an hour the first day he didn't come to play. Serena walked over with Gage and Elizabeth to see what was wrong; before it was over, all the children were in tears. Celey felt like crying herself; even Callie seemed to miss him.

By Thursday, she could no longer stand it. Her little ones were crying for Abner, and she was ready to start howling with them. Celey asked Harrison to hitch up the wagon and load Gage and the twins in the back; they were going to see Abner. She drove to town and picked up Jane, and the older Marcus boys after school let out. The children packed into the wagon bed, and James climbed up next to Celey, smiled, and took the reins. *We've missed you, ma'am.*

Celey felt as if her heart would burst. She loved these loud, rowdy boys who had each found a place in her heart. She felt a sense of awe as she realized she'd come to love their pa too.

George wasn't sure what to do. Abner had cried for four days. Manita's daughter, Topsana, had tried everything to quiet the little boy, but he wouldn't stop. Abner wanted Jane and Celey, and he cried for the kitty, Callie. Daniel had found a neighbor with some kittens hoping Abner would stop crying if he had a kitty; it had taken all day to coax the poor thing out from under the bed where it hid from Abner's screams of *"Not Callie!"* The child would cry until he shuddered and finally fell asleep. When his brothers got home, he was better, but each morning it started again. Abner had never been a difficult child; George wasn't sure what to do. He'd thought about taking him over to Celey's; she'd said he was welcome anytime. George worried that the following day would be worse if he did. He had about decided it would be easier, and he'd get more work done if he just asked her to keep Abner again. Frankly, he was on the verge of begging her.

George looked up from the horse he was shoeing when he heard a wagon enter the yard. The last person he had expected to see was Celey. The bed of her wagon was full of children, his and hers. As soon as James stopped the horses, children were running everywhere. George shaded his eyes from the sun as he looked up at Celey in the wagon. *What is this all about? Did something happen? No,* she replied, *I missed my boys. I hope it's alright that we came.* It took a moment for her words to sink in. When they did, he offered her his hand and said, *I'd say it's about the 'rightest' thing that's happened in several days.*

Epilogue

Abner had refused to let go of Jane when it was time to leave, so Celey had taken him with her. George dropped the older boys off the following day, and the children resumed walking to school together. Abner was happy to see his Pa but hid behind Celey when George started to leave. She assured George that Abner would be no trouble and invited him for supper when he came to pick up the boys.

Every moment they could manage, 'her boys' were at Celey's house. George laughed that he only saw them when he came for supper. After a week of Abner staying at Celey's, George knew he had to say something. He didn't want his son to be unhappy, but he couldn't keep imposing on Celey to care for him.

Celey, I surely do appreciate you taking care of Abner. I was at a loss for what to do, but he will have to come home sometime; it's not right for him to be here all the time. It's not right for my boys to always be here, either. Celey felt her eyes filling with tears. She knew he was right. They were his children, and they should be with their pa. She'd hoped they could all be together, but she could see that George didn't feel the same way. Her ears started to ring as she fought back the tears and thought about the days ahead. She would miss the boys, and oh, what would this do to Jane?

She chose her words carefully, trying not to let the tears spill down her face. *I understand, George. You're right; of course, the boys do need to be with you. It's just..., I thought maybe..., I'll get Abner's things together, and you can take him now if you like.* She turned away to hide that she was crying; George stopped her and said, *Celey, are you listening to me? I asked if you'd consider taking on a houseful of loud, rowdy boys to raise with your children and do me the honor of marrying me.*

They were married a few weeks later, surrounded by their family, friends, and neighbors. Celey had wanted a small ceremony with just the two of them and the children, but Alice insisted that it was high time one of them had a real wedding. After the ceremony, Harrison took both their hands and said, *God always provides.*

Celey noticed that Jane had 'woken up.' She started noticing things again, like wildflowers and shapes in the clouds. She and her cat were always together; wherever Jane and Callie were, so was Abner. The first day the older children left for school, Celey wondered if she was insane. She had three two-year-olds, one screaming for 'his Jane' and two crying for moral support. Thankfully, it only took a few days for Abner to realize that 'his Jane' would come home soon.

Celey watched Jane to see how she was adjusting. Victoria and Joseph had never known their pa, so it wasn't long before she heard them calling George 'Pa' like the other children. Jane always addressed him as 'Sir' or referred to him as 'Abner's pa.' She knew that having all those noisy boys around would be an adjustment, but she thought it might help Jane heal. George's boys loved all her children, but they were especially fond of Jane. George often said that he pitied anyone that mistreated her.

One night, about three months after they married, something happened; Celey knew no matter how long she lived, she would only have to close her eyes to remember it.

The children were all in bed, and it surprised her when Jane stepped into the room. George asked her; *Child, is something wrong?* Jane shook her head but said nothing. George called her to him; it seemed as if it took forever for her to cross the room. When Jane finally stood in front of George, she crawled onto his lap and asked, *May I call you Pa like my brothers do?* Celey's big, gruff husband wrapped his arms around her little girl, a tear running down his cheek, and whispered, *I would be right honored if you did, Darlin'.* George's heart belonged to Jane from that day on.

She and George had worried over many things before God brought them together. But, as Harrison had said He would, God had provided. That night as her husband held <u>their</u> little girl, she had known how much God loved her and that - *love was all that mattered.*

Characters

The Anderson Family

Emily – *daughter of Tom Anderson*

Lem – *brother of Tom Anderson, lives in Missouri*

Tom – *father of Emily, brother of Lem, an associate of Asa Chambers, Sheriff Grady Ellis, Laben Fondren, and Gus Yates*

The Beck Family

Elenore – *daughter of John Beck, wife of Henry Tilman, mother of Rezin*

John – *father of Elenore*

The Buckner Family

Rhoda – *2nd wife of Jacob Dobbs*

The Davis Family

Clarissa - *wife of Harrison Dobbs, mother of Celey, Levi, Amanda, Jackson, and Josiah*

The Dobbs Family

Amanda – *"Mandy" daughter of Harrison and Clarissa (Davis) Dobbs, sister of Celey, Levi, Jackson, and Josiah, wife of Robert Powel, mother of Alexander Powel*

Amos – *son of Jacob and Mahala (Harrison) Dobbs, brother of Ezekiel and Harrison*

Celey – *daughter of Harrison and Clarissa (Davis) Dobbs, sister of Levi, Jackson, Amanda, and Josiah, widow of Daniel Tilman, mother of Jane, Joseph Daniel, and Victoria Abigail Tilman, wife of George Marcus*

Ezekiel – son of Jacob and Mahala (Harrison) Dobbs, brother of Amos and Harrison (twin), father of Jake

Harrison – son of Jacob and Mahala (Harrison) Dobbs, brother of Amos and Ezekiel (twin), widower of Clarissa Davis, father of Celey, Levi. Amanda, Jackson, and Josiah, husband of Serena (Gaylord) Lane, father of Gage and Elizabeth Ann

Jackson – son of Harrison and Clarissa (Davis) Dobbs, brother of Celey, Levi, Amanda, and Josiah

Jacob – "Cap't Jacob," widower of Mahala Harrison, father of Amos, Ezekiel, and Harrison, husband of Rhoda Buckner

Jake – son of Ezekiel, named after his grandfather, "Cap't Jacob"

Levi – son of Harrison and Clarissa (Davis) Dobbs, brother of Celey, Jackson, Amanda, and Josiah, *husband of Melinda Powel, father of Johnathan*

The Harrison Family

Mahala – deceased wife of Jacob Dobbs, mother of Amos, and twins Ezekiel and Harrison

The Lane Family

Peter – *son of William and Serena (Gaylord) Lane*

Serena Gaylord – *widow of William Lane, mother of Peter, wife of Harrison Dobbs, mother of Gage and Elizabeth Ann*

William – *deceased husband of Serena Gaylord, father of Peter*

The Marcus Family

Abner – *son of George and Sarah (Smith) Marcus, brother of James, Thomas, Lewis, and 'Lil' George*

George – *widower of Sarah (Smith), father of Abner, 'Lil' George, James, Lewis, and Thomas, husband of Celey (Dobbs) Tilman*

George – *'Lil' George", son of George and Sarah (Smith) Marcus, brother of James, Thomas, Lewis, and Abner*

James – *son of George and Sarah (Smith) Marcus, brother of Thomas, Lewis, 'Lil' George, and Abner*

Lewis – *son of George and Sarah (Smith) Marcus, brother of James, Thomas, 'Lil' George, and Abner*

Thomas - *son of George and Sarah (Smith) Marcus, brother of James, Lewis, 'Lil' George, and Abner*

The Powel Family

Melinda – *daughter of Newton and Arilla (Wigton) Powel, sister of Robert, wife of Levi Dobbs, mother of Johnathan Dobbs*

Newton – *husband of Arilla Wigton, father of Robert and Melinda*

Robert – *son of Newton and Arilla (Wigton) Powel, brother of Melinda, husband of Amanda Dobbs, father of Alexander*

The Reed Family

Ammon – *son of Caleb and Alice (Tilman)Reed, brother of 'Jazz'*

Caleb – *son of Jasper Reed, husband of Alice Tilman, father of 'Jazz' and Ammon*

Jasper – *father of Caleb and Simon*

Jasper Jefferson 'Jazz' - *son of Caleb and Alice (Tilman) Reed, brother of Ammon*

Simon - *son of Jasper Reed, brother of Caleb*

The Smith Family

Sarah - *wife of George Marcus, mother of James, Thomas, Lewis, 'Lil' George, and Abner*

The Taylor Family

Alsey – *wife of Jefferson Tilman, mother of Daniel, Henry, and Alice.*

The Tilman Family

Alice – *daughter of Jefferson and Alsey (Taylor) Tilman, sister of Daniel and Henry, wife of Celeb Reed, mother of Jasper Jefferson 'Jazz', and Ammon*

Daniel – *son of Jefferson and Alsey (Taylor) Tilman, brother of Henry and Alice, husband of Celey Dobbs, father of Jane, Joseph Daniel, and Victoria Abigail*

Henry – *son of Jefferson and Alsey (Taylor) Tilman, brother of Daniel and Alice, husband of Elenore Beck, father of Rezin*

Jane – *daughter of Daniel and Celey (Dobbs) Tilman, sister of Joseph Daniel and Victoria Abigail*

Jefferson – *husband of Alsey Taylor, father of Daniel, Henry, and Alice*

Joseph Daniel – son of Daniel and Celey (Dobbs) Tilman, brother of Jane and Victoria Abigail

Rezin – *son of Henry and Elenore (Beck) Tilman*

Victoria Abigail – *daughter of Daniel and Celey (Dobbs) Tilman, sister of Jane and Joseph Daniel*

The Wigton Family

Arilla – *wife of Newton Powel, mother of Robert and Melinda*

Waldron, Arkansas Residents

Elam Burel – County Coroner

Mr. & Mrs. Asa Chambers – Mercantile Owners

Judge Collins

Elias Crenshaw

Sheriff Grady Ellis

Abraham Fisher

Laben Fondren

Bird Jeter

Nancy Kennedy

Reverend Logan

Mr. & Mrs. McCollister – Mercantile Owners

Mr. Magruder – Jane's teacher

Carson Murdoch - Lawyer

Doctor Purtle

Samuel Riley

Isaac Turpin

Isaiah Wood

Gus Yates

Little Rock, Arkansas

Monroe S. Hawley - *Governor*

Tackett - *Prison Guard*

United States Marshall Office at Fort Smith

Marshall Hensley

Deputy Jeremiah Hanes

Gabriel Mills, Texas Residents

Manita

Topsana

Baked Pocket Yams

These were "handy" during the winter months and not particular to any one area of the country. Here's how to make them today –

Take several sweet potatoes, individually wrap them in foil, and surround them with mounded hot coals. Occasionally turn the potatoes.

Cook till the sweet steam pipes out of the foil (about 45 minutes). Poke into the potato with a clean sharpened twig to check for doneness (the center will be soft).

When the potatoes are done - *DON'T EAT THEM YET!*

Let them cool a bit, then slip one into each pocket for a hand warmer. These will keep you comfortable while you chat around the campfire.

Pioneer mothers used to send their children off with these in the winter months to keep their hands toasty on the long walk to school. Then the kids would eat them for lunch.

When you eat yours, you might want to use a dish and slather them up with butter.

Cold Biscuit Puddin'

Heat oven to 325°.
Grease the bottom and sides of a 13X9 inch glass baking dish with shortening or cooking spray.
Bake for 1 hour, 5 minutes, and Cool for 30 minutes.
Serve with Brandy Sauce.

Ingredients

4 large eggs

1 large egg yolk

¾ cup sugar

2 ½ cups sweet milk

2 ½ cups of heavy whipping cream

1 tablespoon vanilla

1 tablespoon ground cinnamon

¼ teaspoon salt

10 cups cooked, cold biscuits (day old is best)

½ cup dried cranberries

½ cup diced canned peaches (1/4 inch pieces)

2 tablespoons sugar

½ teaspoon ground cinnamon

2 tablespoons butter

Instructions

In a large bowl, beat 4 whole eggs, 1 egg yolk, and ¾ cup of sugar with a wire whisk until well blended.

Beat in milk, whipping cream, vanilla, 1 tablespoon of ground cinnamon, and ¼ teaspoon salt until well blended.

Stir in 7 cups of bread pieces, cranberries, and peaches. Let stand 20 minutes.

Pour into baking dish. Lightly press the remaining 3 cups of bread pieces on top of the mixture in the baking dish.

In a small bowl, stir 2 tablespoons sugar and ½ teaspoon ground cinnamon until well blended.

Brush the top of the bread mixture with melted 2 tablespoons of butter and sprinkle with cinnamon sugar.

Bake uncovered for 55-65 minutes or until the top is puffed and light golden brown. The Center will jiggle slightly.

Cool for 30 minutes.

Brandy Sauce

Ingredients

½ cup butter

2 tablespoons water

1 large egg

1 cup sugar

2 tablespoons brandy or 1 teaspoon brandy extract

In a 1-quart saucepan, melt ½ cup butter over low heat; do not allow it to simmer.

Remove from heat; cool for 10 minutes.

Mix water and 1 egg in a small bowl; stir into butter until blended.

Stir in 1 cup sugar.

Cook over medium-low heat, constantly stirring, until sugar dissolves and the mixture begins to boil; remove from heat.

Stir in brandy or brandy extract.

Cool for at least 10 minutes before serving.

Serve sauce over warm biscuit puddin'.

Store the remaining dessert and sauce, covered, in the refrigerator.

Other Titles Available

<u>*Fiction*</u>

Emma: Heritage Series- Volume I

A real-life Cinderella story - complete with a wicked stepmother. - "Emma lay very still, her eyes tightly closed. Sometimes - if she concentrated - she could make out her Momma's face. She was the youngest child of eighteen. She had barely been two when her beloved Momma died. Losing Momma had hurt Papa deeply. No one had wanted him to be sad, but why did *she* have to be their new mother?" Based on the author's great-grandmother and events in her life, much of the story is fiction. However, threads of reality are woven throughout Emma's story. The real-life Emma was the youngest in a family of eighteen children. As to the rest, it is up to the reader to decide, fact or fiction.

Lone Star Literary Life Review

"It wasn't age or distance that mattered – love was all that mattered."

"Emma by Susan Diane Black Blackmon is the first in the Heritage Series. With a strong historical foundation, this fiction flows like a traditional fairy tale that has both dark and light elements, providing readers with an early 1900s Texas narrative, a sweet romance, and an evil stepmother.

Blackmon's writing style is clean and uncomplicated, making Emma an ideal choice for readers of all ages, including middle-grade and young adult readers who enjoy an interesting

Texas fiction based on real-life people and events.

Emma can rightly be likened to Cinderella. However, this story resembles Little House on the Prairie by Laura Ingalls Wilder as well, with the very act of survival in a harsh land during a harsh time providing more than enough turmoil, hardship, and even celebrations, such as box socials and courtship. Add a woman who chooses to destroy others to satisfy her avarice, and Emma quickly becomes a modest yet powerful parable and cautionary tale. Rising above and even overcoming wickedness will always resonate with readers as relatable and meaningful, with Blackmon nimbly delivering the effective trope of good versus evil and so much more in this first fascinating book in the Heritage Series."

"This was such a heartwarming read. As the description states, it's based on a Cinderella-like story, but there are many more layers to this story. You won't regret this one!"

"Loved the story....had a hard time putting it down...I am looking forward to the next edition."

"This book kept me wanting to know what was going to happen next. Emma made me laugh and cry. I read it in one day. I cannot wait to read the next book."

"I am delighted how the story was a page-turner and hard to put down. Emma's story is very heart-warming and real-life Cinderella indeed. The details of the narrative are on point as well. I love this one very much."

Available 2023

Melinda: Heritage Series -Volume III

*The story of Melinda Powel and Levi
Dobbs. From the letters written by the
people who inspired the characters
during the Civil War in Texas.*

Nonfiction

Daniel Brown Boultinghouse
&
Mary Jane Russell
A Collection of Civil War Letters
and
Family Documents
With Genealogical and Historical
Commentary

The real-life family of Emma And Celey

ᏣᏍᏣᏍᏣᏍᏣᏍᏣᏍᏣᏍᏣᏍᏣ

Genealogy

The Giles Driver Family
A Compilation of the Descendants of Giles Driver
Isle of Wight, Virginia
Volume I

The Giles Driver Family
A Compilation of the Descendants of Giles Driver
Isle of Wight, Virginia
Volume II

CHEROKEECHEROKEECHEROKEECHEROKEECHEROKEE

Whispers from the Past…..
Buytenhuys to Boultinghouse
Volume I
Immigration, Canadian Kin, & Migration

Whispers from the Past…..
Buytenhuys to Boultinghouse
Volume II
The Descendants of Daniel Boultinghouse 1797-
1867

CHEROKEECHEROKEECHEROKEECHEROKEECHEROKEE

For more information, contact:
Susan Black Blackmon
susan@whispersfromthepast.net
whispersfromthepast.net
grandmastrunk.net

Author's Amazon Page –
https://www.amazon.com/author/sblackmon

---

www.ingramcontent.com/pod-product-compliance
Lightning Source LLC
Chambersburg PA
CBHW030355030726
47497CB00002B/344